# A TUSCAN SUMMER

*Recent Titles by Sally Stewart from Severn House*

APPOINTMENT IN VENICE
CASTLES IN SPAIN
CURLEW ISLAND
THE DAISY CHAIN
FLOODTIDE
JOURNEYS' END
LOST AND FOUND
MOOD INDIGO
OVER THE SEA TO SKYE
POSTCARDS FROM A STRANGER
PROSPERO'S DAUGHTERS
A RARE BEAUTY
ROMAN SPRING
A TIME TO DANCE
TRAVELLING GIRL
A TUSCAN SUMMER

# A TUSCAN SUMMER

## Sally Stewart

This first world edition published 2010
in Great Britain and in 2011 in the USA by
SEVERN HOUSE PUBLISHERS LTD of
9–15 High Street, Sutton, Surrey, England, SM1 1DF.
Trade paperback edition first published
in Great Britain and the USA 2011 by
SEVERN HOUSE PUBLISHERS LTD.

British Library Cataloguing in Publication Data

Stewart, Sally, 1930–
    A Tuscan summer.
    1. Vacations – Italy – Tuscany – Fiction. 2. Real estate
    Development – Italy – Tuscany – Prevention – Fiction.
    I. Title
    823.9'14–dc22

ISBN-13: 978-0-7278-6966-1   (cased)
ISBN-13: 978-1-84751-295-6   (trade paper)

Except
describe
publicati
is purely

*All Seve*

Severn I
the lead
are prin

g

ns

uncil [FSC],
our titles that
ry the FSC logo.

FSC   Product group from well-managed
forests and other controlled sources
www.fsc.org  Cert no. SA-COC-1565
© 1996 Forest Stewardship Council

Typeset by Palimpsest Book Production Ltd.,
Falkirk, Stirlingshire.
Printed and bound in Great Britain by the
MPG Books Group, Bodmin, Cornwall.

# One

It was strange but oddly satisfying; she'd committed a sort of murder, and Mrs Eleanor Fanshawe was no more. The face now staring back at her in the mirror confirmed it, seeming to confirm that at least some of the mistakes of the past three years might have been laid to rest as well.

Considering them, Nell reckoned that all the saints in heaven must know how hard she'd tried to be trendy, seized every new fad and fashion in her feverish determination not to be left too far behind. But none of it had done a particle of good. Borne upwards on the wings of ever-mounting success, Giles had floated steadily away from her. In the brief span of their marriage – such a lovely marriage they'd meant it to be – the ambitious young lawyer she'd fallen in love with had more than fulfilled his brilliant promise; as a specialist in international law, he was now always in demand and endlessly in motion.

Whenever there was time to remember that he had a wife and home, he returned too tired to conceal impatience with a woman who disliked the way their life had changed. She still wanted to toil, in house and garden – humdrum work they should be paying duller people to do. She was supposed to be joining in the rich, full life enjoyed by every other wife he knew, not being a domestic slave. Anxious to please, Nell had done her best. But when she'd sprained her ankle in the aerobics class, fallen off several disdainful horses in Richmond Park, and crawled home a nervous wreck after a lacerating round of neighbourhood bridge parties, the writing was clearly on the wall: the rich, full life was not for her. She paid off the hired help and went thankfully back to working for herself. Giles watched and shrugged, and then went off to his next foreign appointment, leaving the sting of failure behind – she'd let him down again.

The worse grief of the past three years had been their lack of children. A family, of course, he'd said at the beginning of their marriage, but not yet – better to wait until his feet were firmly on the ladder of success. But the time still wasn't right, and now she feared that it never would be. He'd seen too many well-ordered adult lives reduced to chaos by parenthood to be tempted into it himself.

Denied what she'd wanted so much, Nell began to write books for other people's children. The varied adventures, in particular, of a small black bear called Seb had proved so unexpectedly popular that the publishers had begged for more. Nell was happy writing and illustrating the stories, but she worked on them only when Giles was away. She knew that her success irritated him more than failure would have done – she'd succeeded, but at the wrong thing, apparently.

Still observing the face in the mirror, she considered it as impartially as she could. Not much to brag about – too thin for beauty, too wide of mouth and stubborn of chin – but at least it belonged to a woman she could recognize again. The improbable gold streaks had been washed out of her brown hair, purple or glitter eyeshadow thrown away, and clothes with attitude bundled up for delivery to Oxfam. It was time to face the truth: if her ship of happiness was going down, she must sink with it as herself, not as the fashionable fraud the glossy, terrifying women around her had seen through with such ease.

She nodded sombrely at her reflection in the mirror, then smiled at it as the front doorbell rang – Jonathan, no doubt, without a latchkey once again. Her much-loved younger brother might be a rising star in the frenetic world of stage design, but an organized householder he was not. In theory, he lived in the self-contained basement flat downstairs, but, more often than not, the necessities of life could only be found in his sister's part of the house upstairs.

'You could stay and share supper with me,' she suggested as he stepped into the hall. 'Nothing fancy: just watercress soup, roast lamb, and some cheese afterwards.'

Jonathan looked surprised at the invitation. 'With *you*, not you and Giles? I thought he was due home today.'

'I thought so too – my simple menu was meant to be a relief after two weeks of living it up in Brussels. But he's gone to Italy instead. His secretary remembered to ring and tell me, but not until I'd already put the lamb in the oven.'

Jonathan studied his sister for a moment, decided not to point out that Giles might have managed an earlier telephone call himself, and selected something else it seemed safer to comment on.

'You look different – dare I say it to a woman of your advancing years? – but younger somehow. It's the hair, I think . . . you've got rid of the streaky bits.'

'Highlights, if you please, not streaky bits,' she insisted firmly, 'but I thought "au naturel" would make a change. Now, come and talk to me in the kitchen. I want to hear how *Aida* is going to look this time round. Any camels or elephants on stage for the Grand March?'

Jonathan was safely diverted to his favourite subject. 'No, thank God: the Royal Opera House doesn't go in for performing live-stock, and for once the director is putting his trust in Verdi's music – no gimmicks; in fact, no postmodernist mayhem at all. It's going to be rather good, I think.'

Nell smiled at the understatement, aware from it that her brother reckoned they had an artistic triumph on their hands. Thereafter while they ate, she kept the conversation on matters operatic and wrangled amicably with him over the rival merits of Italian versus home-grown sopranos. They talked, too, of their absent parents, now settling into a new diplomatic posting in Moscow, and that led them to remembering the grandmother who had brought them up instead, while her daughter and son-in-law spent all their time serving abroad.

Born in the foothills of the Apennines, Francesca Pizzoni, as she then was, had married an Englishman who'd brought her to live for the rest of her life in London. The separation from her family and Tuscan home had been complete, and her grandchildren had grown tired of asking why they weren't ever taken to meet their Italian relatives. '*E finita, quella vita,*' was all Francesca would say; '*siamo qui adesso, non è vero?*' But she made sure that Nell and Jonathan learned to speak her mother tongue as easily as they spoke English, and she taught them all she could of her homeland's culture, traditions and heart-stopping beauty.

It was Jonathan who referred to her now. 'I know it's three years since Nonna died, but we still miss her, don't we?' He'd never put the conviction into words but had always thought it was Francesca's sudden death that had driven Nell into a hasty marriage; she'd wanted someone else to love. 'It's too late now,' he said suddenly, 'but why didn't we insist on knowing more than the bare bones of the story? She was a teenager living on her father's farm, and the Pizzonis did what so many Italian families bravely did – sheltered an escaped English prisoner-of-war. But she never even told us where the place was.'

'And after the war our grandfather, by then a qualified doctor, went back to thank his Italian friends,' said Nell, going on with what they knew of the story. 'The schoolgirl he remembered had grown up and grown beautiful. Naturally enough, they fell in love, and he brought her back to England.' She hesitated over what to say next. 'It's all Nonna ever told us, and I think we were meant to assume that, while we were growing up, the Pizzoni family died out. Now I doubt if that was true. When I finally made myself go through her things a little while ago, I found a bundle of letters in her desk that she'd sent to a place called Pratolino. Each one had been returned unopened – presumably by her father; they were addressed to Luigi Pizzoni.'

'It doesn't make sense, does it?' Jonathan asked after a moment's thought. 'Why would a man who'd risked his own life to shelter Grandfather disown his daughter afterwards for marrying that same *Inglesi*? Poor darling Nonna, though – what a sod Luigi must have been to treat her like that. A brave sod, but a sod all the same.'

Then Jonathan waved the sad little story away. With Francesca dead, they'd never know what had happened all those years ago. Better now to talk about something he *could* get to the bottom of, and he gently lifted a strand of his sister's soft brown hair.

'Why the different look, Nell? I like it better, as a matter of fact, but I'd got used to the ultra-fashionable Mrs Fanshawe!'

She was tempted to make up some trivial reason, but he lived too near to her to have missed the signs of strain in her marriage, and she couldn't ever lie to him.

'I decided to have done with pretending,' she finally admitted. 'It was an amusing game at first, making myself into someone else. But it's become a game that Giles takes seriously: the Nell

Ashley he married won't quite do any more. Instead of cooking spaghetti *alle vongole* for him at home, we must eat in expensive restaurants. I suppose I can manage that, but I *can't* jump into bed with any rich man who might give him another push up the ladder, and I refuse to look the other way when the bored wives we meet signal to my very attractive husband that they're his for the taking.'

'So you're going back to being the girl he fell in love with,' Jonathan said quietly. 'Throwing down a challenge to Giles, in fact. It's risky, love.'

'Oh, I realize that, but it's now or never, I think. He's in desperate need of a rest, and we'd planned to go away when he got back from Brussels . . . Find some green and peaceful place where we could walk in clean air and get used to talking to each other again. That was going to be challenge enough, but, after this afternoon's telephone call, I realized that if he doesn't still want me as I really am, then our marriage has to come to an end.' She managed a wry smile at the concern in her brother's face. 'Sorry . . . I didn't mean to burden you with all that, but you did ask!'

Not given to demonstrations of affection, Jonathan merely leaned over and patted her hand. 'The shoulder to cry on is always available,' he said, 'but I'm betting that it won't be needed. When the chips are down, Giles will see what he risks losing. I'm a trifle partial, of course, but I reckon that my dear skin and blister ought to be enough for *any* man.'

'And what brother could say fairer than that?' Nell murmured, touched by a tribute that was all the sweeter for coming from a young man who made it a point of honour to resist the extravagant language of the theatre. Then she sounded her usual calm self again. 'I'll let you know about going away – no need to feed the cat or the canary we haven't got; just keep an eye on things, if you will, please.'

Jonathan agreed that he would, thanked her for the supper he hadn't had to cook himself, and disappeared downstairs to his basement flat, promising to try not to lose his door-key while she was away. She didn't see anything more of him for the next couple of days but knew that, with an opening night in the offing, he would be crawling back in the small hours, if not actually sleeping backstage at Covent Garden.

But Giles did come home, only a few hours later than she'd been told to expect him. He looked even more tired than when he'd gone away, and she sensed at once that something she didn't yet know about made him preoccupied enough to not even notice the demise of Mrs Eleanor Fanshawe. But it seemed not to matter now, because whatever filled his mind was more important. When supper was nearly over, she wearied suddenly of their polite small talk and tried to make the conversation real.

'Dear Giles, you look ready to drop. Please go to bed and sleep, but just say first that we *can* still have the holiday you need so badly.'

He poured more wine into their glasses before answering. 'The holiday is certainly on, but not quite in the way we planned. What would you think of a couple of months, not weeks, spent in a splendid Tuscan villa instead? Better than a rainy fortnight in the Highlands?'

'It might be,' she said cautiously, 'although I quite like rain myself. But I suspect a catch somewhere. I'd like to know a little more about the change of plan. Is it why you suddenly went to Italy?' She saw him nod, and went on herself before he could answer. 'Don't, please, tell me that the villa in Tuscany is Frank Middleton's idea.'

Giles stretched out his hand and caught hold of hers, now agitatedly sweeping up crumbs on the table.

For once, instead of getting cross at her patent dislike of his firm's most high-profile client, he answered gently. 'Let me tell you what's been happening. Frank was taken ill in Brussels – only a slight heart attack, but a warning nevertheless that he must slow down for a bit. It was enough to bring forward something he's had in mind for a while that could be combined with us all having a rest and a good time in Italy.'

'If that means sharing the villa with *him*, then the answer's no, Giles; I'll take a Scottish deluge any day.' The flat refusal didn't surprise him and he went on as if she hadn't spoken.

'The villa's owned by Count Vittorio Guidi. He lives in one wing of it still; the rest he's prepared to rent out. That's why I went there – to arrange things with him. He's a charming, rather ineffectual man who's somehow got left behind in the rush to overhaul rural Italy.'

Nell sipped the wine she'd been given, wondering if there could be two more different men on earth than an old-fashioned Italian aristocrat and the power-hungry, self-made plutocrat that was still Frank Middleton, even if he had been knighted for his services to industry.

'I can see why you were needed to deal with the Count,' she said finally, 'and I'm sorry about the heart attack, but Sir Frank has a wife – downtrodden though she may be – and a daughter to keep him company; at least I suppose Jacqueline will be there?'

Giles frowned at the acid note in Nell's voice but still didn't take issue with it, knowing that his position was weak. 'There'll be other guests as well,' he admitted; 'a high-powered French architect and his rather supercilious wife. Taken in conjunction with servants who only speak Italian, they'll be more than poor Joan Middleton can manage. Frank needs me there, Nell, and she will need you. I know it isn't what we planned, but the place is beautiful beyond words and I thought you always wanted to visit Tuscany.'

Ignoring that for the moment, Nell went back to how the conversation had begun. 'You mentioned two months there – wouldn't that be rather excessive, from every point of view? The firm would surely think so.'

Driven into being completely honest at last, Giles shook his head. 'They know there's work involved as well. The Count has land lying idle. What were once vineyards and productive olive trees are neglected now, and farm buildings are falling into ruin as the country people give up and find work in the cities. Frank's idea is to persuade the Count to let him redevelop the estate into a holiday complex of a very superior kind, but there's a lot of negotiating and planning to be done.'

He saw the expression on Nell's face and hurried on. 'All right, you don't like the idea – want the old way of life to continue unchanged. But it won't, Nell; the days when the *contadini* were content to work from dawn to sunset in order to scrape a living are over, and Count Guidi knows that as well as Frank Middleton does. This would at least give the place a future.'

There was a long silence in the room before he spoke again. 'I can't make you go to Tuscany, but I must go myself; I've promised Frank and I can't let him down. I know you don't like him,

Nell, and he intimidates people when he can, but that's the way
he gets things done, and there's no escaping the fact that he's a
genius in his own way. I wouldn't let him bully *you*, and it would
at least mean that we'd see more of each other than we have for
months past – all my fault, I know, not yours.'

'Emotional blackmail,' Nell said with a wry smile; 'not fair
at all. All right, I'll go to Tuscany, Giles, but on certain conditions. I'm not going as Joan Middleton's housekeeper – I'll take
my own work to do. I won't be patronized by a haughty
Parisienne, and if I hate what Frank Middleton proposes to do
with the Count's estate, I shall feel free to tell him so. Those
are my terms.'

After an astonished moment Giles nodded at her. 'Accepted, Nell.'
But he still looked puzzled and stared at his wife more closely. 'I
think I've missed something – you've got the bit between your
teeth, and it sounds as if F.M. might be in for a rough ride. Remember
the heart attack, please, when you start to lay about you!'

She could smile at him now, thinking that it was the first time
he'd spoken lightly of his paymaster. 'I'll be sweetness itself if I
can. Now, that's enough talk for tonight. You *must* go and get
into bed while I clear up here.'

He was beyond arguing, but his tired mind still registered some
alteration that it seemed important to pin down. Then he realized what it was – he'd suddenly been reminded of the girl he'd
met for the first time in a supermarket car park three years earlier.
He'd teased her afterwards for literally scraping an acquaintance
with him when her laden trolley had run down a slope and gouged
out a scratch along the side of his cherished car. He could still
remember being too angry to accept with any grace at all the
apology and offer to pay for the repair that she'd at once made.
Then, affronted in her turn, she'd suggested that he could avoid
more damage in future by coming to the supermarket at a different
time. He was there the following week to find her and make his
own apology. They'd laughed together then, and fallen in love.

He smiled now at the memory, but his last sleepy thought
almost brought him awake again. It looked like being an interesting stay in Tuscany, but he remembered, alas, that interesting
times were what the Chinese wished on their enemies as a curse!

# Two

Breakfast began peacefully enough the next morning. Giles predicted a frantic day in chambers in Gracechurch Street, clearing his desk for a longer absence than he'd anticipated. The next morning he must meet Lady Middleton off a train from the north and lodge her in a hotel for the night. On the day following, he, and Nell of course, would shepherd her to Tuscany – she was a nervous traveller and needed looking after.

'Can't her daughter do that?' Nell enquired.

'Jacqueline is in Brussels, keeping Frank quiet until the medics say he's fit to travel to Italy. She's the only one who can; he takes no notice of his wife, understandably enough.' Giles saw Nell's lifted eyebrow and gave a little shrug. 'All right, it sounds unkind. But you've met her once; that's enough to know that she's a dull, dowdy woman born to be overlooked.'

'Not "born to be",' Nell said with sudden sharpness. 'She's been destroyed by living for twenty years with an overbearing bully of a husband, and now you sound as contemptuous of her as he is.'

Giles abandoned Joan Middleton to fly to the defence of his client. 'Whereas you, on the other hand, despise *him* because he hasn't had the time or inclination to acquire the social graces you think are important.'

Nell's flash of anger turned to sudden sadness. 'I don't despise the man, Giles; I fear him. He damages people or, at the very least, changes them; I'm afraid he's even changing you. I wish he'd never picked you out of Marchants' team to do his endless work for him.'

There was a little pause before she got an answer, delivered this time with a cool politeness that defeated her. 'You're creating a monster that doesn't exist. Frank wraps his family in the luxury he's earned for them, and now you and I are being invited to share in it, too; let's try to enjoy it, shall we?'

He got up to leave the room, but something in her attitude

made him hesitate on his way to the door, and he dropped a kiss on her hair as he went past. The gesture was enough to win a smile from her.

'Well, if Tuscan luxury is on offer, I must buy some summer clothes before I close up the house and leave the garden tidy. You're not the only one with a lot to do if we must be ready to leave the day after tomorrow.'

The change of tone in her voice made his expression relax, and he was Giles again, the man she knew and loved.

'I know it's a rush, Nell, but thank you for agreeing to come. We need you there for much more than trying to make ourselves understood!'

But when the moment for departure came, he had to set off for Italy without her. Jonathan had been hurt at the Opera House the evening before, and Nell had no option but to wait and see her brother safely home from hospital with a broken arm in plaster. She left two days later, with friends organized to keep an eye on him and her anxiety about him over.

At Pisa airport her instructions were to find Giles, not board the rail link connecting it with Florence. But the only person she recognized in the arrivals lounge was Frank Middleton, his bulky figure unmistakable among the smaller Italians around him.

With fear clutching her heart, she just managed a greeting before asking why Giles wasn't there. The question was waved aside.

'Urgent business, Mrs Fanshawe, that's all. These people here do nothing but have public holidays – there's another one tomorrow, so Giles had to attend to something today. No need to worry about him – he's in good fettle.'

Without even trying, Nell thought, Middleton had made their position clear: she and her husband were there to be useful, not as guests. So much for the holiday Giles needed so badly. But at least anger burned away whatever nervousness she might have felt in the company of this large and intimidating man. She watched as he signalled to the porter guarding her luggage and then led the way outside into warmth and blinding sunlight. A car was parked near the exit and its small, thin-faced driver was holding one of the doors open.

'His name's Giuseppe,' Middleton said, 'but, for some reason known only to himself, we have to call him Beppe. Doesn't speak a word of English, and nor does his wife.'

'So inconsiderate of them,' Nell murmured, and then held out her hand to the waiting servant.

'*Buon giorno, Beppe. Io sono Signora Fanshawe, la moglie del Signor Giles.*'

'*Lo so, Signora, e buon giorno anche a Lei.*' A dazzling smile had lit his face at the sound of his own language, and he handed her tenderly into the car, apparently not concerned that it left the *padrone* to fend for himself. Nell heard a grunt of disapproval beside her and decided that it would be a tactful moment to enquire about her host's health.

'Nothing wrong with me,' he said, as she'd guessed he would. 'Fool doctors running up large bills as usual, that's all.' Then, aware that she'd twice surprised him already, Middleton turned to look at her. 'Giles said you spoke the lingo, but I thought he meant you could manage phrasebook stuff. It's obviously more than that.'

Nell made her explanation as brief as possible. 'My brother and I were brought up by our Italian grandmother, and she made sure we learned her own tongue. I'm glad she did – it's a lovely language.'

'I'm not saying it won't come in useful,' her companion admitted. 'My wife can't even understand the servants' sign language, much less what they say.' That dealt with, he gestured to the busy noontime traffic around them – another source of irritation, apparently. 'Look at them, all knocking off for a couple of hours so that they can go home to lunch.'

'It is the custom of the country,' Nell pointed out gently; 'rather a civilized one, I think.'

She felt rather than saw the glance this earned for her, and realized at the same time that crossing swords with this autocrat beside her was something she might actually come to enjoy. Perhaps for his wife's sake, she should go on as she'd started; at least it could do him no harm to have to fight his corner for a change, instead of trampling over the opposition.

Then, as if he'd read what was in her mind, he attacked from a different quarter. 'You're not today's only arrival; our French guests are coming off the night train from Paris – Bertrand and

Sylvie de la Tour. My daughter went to meet them, taking Giles to his meeting at the same time. She's very involved in what I'm doing here, so it's a good thing they get on so well together – they'll be seeing a lot of each other.'

Nell nodded politely but didn't answer. Baulked in that direction, Middleton abandoned finesse and settled for bluntness instead. 'I get the feeling from Giles that you don't reckon much to my Italian scheme, Mrs Fanshawe. Am I right about that? It doesn't matter either way, of course, but I like to know where I stand with people.'

She supposed she was meant to flounder between an embarrassed confession and an outright lie. After a moment she was able to smile at him. 'I scarcely know what your scheme is, Sir Frank, but if it entails covering the Tuscan countryside with opulent holiday houses and swimming pools, then you're right: I don't reckon much to it at all.'

His bright eyes gleamed with what he was going to say next. 'Honestly spoken, but I hope you'll admit as well that I'm not a man who makes business mistakes. Happen *I'll* be the one who's proved right, not a romantic like you.'

'You'll be the one who will win,' she agreed; 'I'm not sure if that amounts to the same thing.'

She was surprised by a dry bark that she identified as her companion laughing. 'You're not only honest, you're a fighter as well; Giles didn't warn me about that. Reckoned I'd find it out for myself, I expect.'

He'd realized also that she was intelligent – a combination he didn't expect to come across very often in women. If she'd been beautiful as well, he might have been anxious, but she was a thin, understated sort of girl – almost plain, in fact. Giles's wife wasn't what he'd expected, but he could see now that she wouldn't get in his way. The thought almost made him give her hand a consolatory pat – he respected a worthy loser – but he pointed out instead that, after they'd skirted Florence, they'd be at Poggione and the Villa Guidi in no time.

Once the towers and domes of the city's skyline were left behind, they climbed steadily out of the river valley into the foothills of the Apennines. The narrow silver ribbon of the Arno was still visible, but Nell's eyes were fixed on the nearer view.

She was remembering her grandmother's descriptions of Tuscany – a landscape ordered and made abundantly fruitful by the generations that had lived and died there. Too hilly for machines, the land had had to be tilled for wheat and maize with wooden ploughs drawn by the beautiful white oxen of Tuscany – Chianina or Maremmana – whose horns were garlanded with crimson tassels at *vendemmia*-time. The vines and olives that clothed the steeper slopes were tended by hand, and dotted among them were the cypress-guarded, russet-roofed *poderi* where the farmers and their families lived. Castles, often empty even within Nonna's memory, crowned the wooded hilltops, and above *them* floated the misty blue mountains themselves against a Tuscan sky. Not like English skies, Francesca had insisted, even though she'd grown to love those as well.

Nell thought Nonna would still have recognized her homeland, but there were changes that would have saddened her. Some of the farm buildings were derelict, and, however beautiful they looked in the late-May sunshine, the wildflowers everywhere spoke of land that was no longer being worked.

Poggione, when they drove through it, wasn't the village Nell had expected, but a small town with elegantly arcaded piazza, church, trattoria, and the indispensable bar whose pavement terrace was the local meeting place even this early in the year. It looked a convivial, thriving little town, where shoppers would go every day for fresh food and fresh gossip.

'That, at least, is encouraging,' Nell said, thinking aloud; 'there are still people enough around to keep Poggione busy.'

'For the moment,' the Job's comforter beside her agreed, 'but how many youngsters do you see? How many children?' Then, as they left the network of streets behind, he gestured to the terraced slopes they were driving through.

'This is Guidi land still. The family owned most of Poggione itself until the old Count – Vitttorio's grandfather – sold it off bit by bit to make the villa fit to live in.'

Nell looked at the beautifully tended vine rows and the olive trees in spring leaf, and wondered for how much longer they would be there.

Again, Middleton seemed to guess what was in her mind. 'This isn't what I'm after – it's too high, too hilly. The winters are fierce up here when the *tramontana*'s blowing. But Guidi's estate stretches round this mountain flank in front of us and runs down into a wide, sheltered valley. That's where I'll build as soon as Giles has got the legal business tidied away.'

'Does the Count mind much?' Nell asked for something to say.

'How can he? He knows as well as I do that things have to change. But God knows how *much* he minds – the man spends his time writing poetry.'

The disgust in Middleton's voice would have made Nell smile at any other time, but not now. She doubted whether the ferociously single-minded tycoon beside her would have been careful to spell out his intentions to the gentle aristocrat Giles had described. Wealth corrupted as surely as power did, and Middleton hadn't become phenomenally successful by being scrupulous in his business dealings.

She might have felt obliged to say so if Beppe hadn't then diverted her attention by turning off the road into a wood-bordered lane. It led them past a stone farmhouse and outbuildings and then through an archway into a paved courtyard. Old terracotta urns planted with neatly clipped box bordered a central, water-lily-covered pool where a bronze Pan piped a tinkling cascade of water music.

The house now facing them was beautiful, with roses clambering over a façade whose stucco had faded to the softest apricot. Small side wings held out protecting arms, seeming to enfold it in quietness and grace.

Nell scrambled out of the car and stood looking at it in silence until Middleton came to stand beside her.

'Giles said it was lovely,' she murmured, 'but words can't describe it.' Then she offered her host a smile he hadn't seen before. 'I can't regret Scotland any more! Thank you for letting us come.'

Then the wide front door was opened and the woman Nell remembered from their London meeting walked down the shallow flight of steps to meet them. She smiled nervously at the first of the day's arrivals. At least this one was sure to speak English, but Joan Middleton's mind held the image of Eleanor Fanshawe, met once in an expensive restaurant – elegant and sophisticated.

It was hard to reconcile that memory with the simply dressed girl who now smiled as if she was happy to be there.

While Beppe carried Nell's luggage into the house, Lady Middleton hurriedly explained that the others weren't back yet. Jacqueline had telephoned to say that the train from Paris was arriving late – she and Giles were waiting for it still. The poor woman sounded defensive, Nell thought, as if anything that might irritate her husband was somehow always her fault.

It was a relief when they were interrupted by a short, plump servant introduced to Nell as Lucia, Beppe's wife, cook-housekeeper and general mainstay of the villa. She smiled as her husband had done at being addressed in Italian, and firmly announced that *she* would conduct the English guest to her bedroom.

Led up a beautiful curving staircase that only the eighteenth century could have produced, Nell was given a helpful summary of how the villa worked. *Il Signor Conte* still lived in one wing, of course, looked after by a manservant called Fabio. She, Beppe and their daughter, Carlotta, were in the other wing; the main house in between was for the paying guests.

Their son, Gianni, and his family lived in the farmhouse beyond the courtyard, tended the vines and olives, and produced the food and livestock the household needed. Once launched, Lucia was happy to stay and talk, and only by hinting tactfully that she was tired from travelling could Nell lead her to suggest that the signora must rest and await the return of her *caro marito*.

Nell was sitting by the window when Giles walked into the room an hour later. Clothes unpacked and hung up, she was drinking in a view that seemed the epitome of Tuscany.

'Long time no see,' he said as he bent down to kiss her. 'It's a pleasure to have you here at last, Mrs Fanshawe.'

'The pleasure's all mine, I'm sure,' she replied in kind, then added seriously, 'I mean it, Giles. This is a paradisal place, and even finding F.M. at the airport instead of you wasn't unbearable. I decided that a policy of polite resistance is the way to deal with him, and if I do nothing else while I'm here, I mean to teach it to Joan Middleton.'

Giles grinned but shook his head. 'You were going to remember the heart attack, I thought! Don't underrate him, Nell; he's a hard man to cross.'

She didn't argue the point and asked about the French couple instead.

'Very French,' Giles said, 'and well-regarded in high places, we're to understand. The lady has just finished redesigning rooms in the Elysee Palace, no less. Our poor hostess is going to need help with *her*, I'm afraid.'

'And the legal business you had to see to – all tidied away?'

'No, because the time of the meeting had been stupidly screwed up – I wasn't expected until after the weekend. But at least it meant that Jacqueline didn't have to kick her heels alone in Florence for several hours.'

Nell told herself not to become paranoid about her host. He might well manipulate an appointment, but even he couldn't hold back a train on its way from Paris. She returned to looking at the view while Giles changed out of formal clothes, and then suggested a walk before dinner.

'Tell me something first, please,' she asked when he agreed. 'Is Count Guidi really aware of what the Middleton plan is going to amount to, or has it been discussed in such vague terms that he thinks the estate is merely exchanging an owner who can no longer afford it for one who can?'

Giles frowned at a question he hadn't been prepared for. 'The Count understands English, and he isn't a halfwit, any more than Frank is a villain. The terms of the negotiation have been made perfectly clear. If you don't trust my client, you might at least trust me; I'm as involved in it as he is.'

'That's my only comfort,' Nell said, 'the fact that you *are* involved. Now, let's forget why we're here – I'm longing to explore the garden.'

'*D'accordo,* Signora! Thanks to Beppe, my Italian is coming on apace – I may soon be able to fathom at least half of what he says. Meanwhile, I *can* lead you to the *giardino* without a single false step. But if you're expecting a well-tended English affair, forget it now; it's more wilderness than garden.'

He was right, Nell discovered, but what a beautiful wilderness it turned out to be – a riotous tangle of shrubs and flowers that clambered over terrace walls and even spread across the paths they walked on. Someone *had* loved it, she felt sure, and placed with care the benches and charming pieces of statuary that were now almost submerged in greenery. Old-fashioned roses and lavender run wild scented the air, and in this enchanted oasis even the songbirds had found a refuge from the Italian mania for shooting anything that flew.

'You can't see it from this level,' Giles explained, 'but there's a swimming pool a little lower down, in a sort of grotto protected from the winds. I haven't tried it yet, but Jacqueline's already been in – she's a redoubtable girl. I think you'll think so too when you meet her.'

Nell didn't answer and gestured instead to what stretched in front of them. 'My grandmother must have known a view like this; she described it so exactly. Imagine how hard it would have been to accustom herself to life in London.'

'I grant you that,' Giles said gently, 'but you must also imagine what her life might have been like here. Don't romanticize this lovely place, Nell; its climate is harsh compared with ours, and its land can only be worked with back-breaking manual labour.' He looked at his watch and then pulled her to her feet. 'Time we went indoors, I think, and got spruced up for dinner. You'll have to fly the flag for England. Vittorio Guidi is invited as well, and my guess is that Sylvie de la Tour will be reckoning to knock his eye out with Parisian chic!'

'I doubt if he'd even notice,' said Nell. 'According to our host, he only concerns himself with poetry.' She paused and then added a thoughtful rider. 'In any case, I think it's the "redoubtable" girl I might have to watch.' Then, with a faint smile, she led the way back to the house.

Giles followed, wondering whether he imagined that Italy was already having an effect on his wife when they were only at the beginning of their visit. He felt disinclined to imagine how it might end. Beppe had a phrase – *che sara, sara* – for whenever an outcome seemed in doubt. Said with his customary shrug, it meant that they were playthings in the hands of Fate. But Giles still clung to an inborn belief in self-determination, despite a pricking in his thumbs that warned him of where they were – in an ancient legend-haunted land where anything might happen. A rational Anglo-Saxon approach to life quite possibly wasn't on the cards here at all.

# Three

Downstairs an hour later, they found Beppe, now dressed for evening duties in black trousers and an immaculate white jacket, trying to explain to the *padrona* why he should serve pre-dinner drinks in the *salone* and not on the terrace. She gave a little sigh of relief at the sight of the only guest she needed, and Nell felt a wave of pity for a woman who so clearly wished herself to be anywhere but where she was.

'He keeps twitching,' Joan Middleton said despairingly. 'What is that supposed to mean?'

Trying not to smile, Nell suggested that Beppe was pretending to shiver. 'He thinks you'll find it too cool outside now and suggests aperitifs in here. If you agree, Lady Middleton, you need only say, "*D'accordo, Beppe; grazie*".'

When the phrase had been repeated haltingly and a smiling servant had returned to the kitchen, Joan Middleton's strained face relaxed a little.

'It sounds so easy . . . and so pretty, too,' she said wistfully. 'My husband thinks a phrase book is all that's needed but . . .' She left that sentence unfinished and started again. 'I mustn't keep asking you to help, Mrs Fanshawe – Eleanor, I should say – but just having you here makes a difference.' She tried to smile but the little break in her voice hinted at more strain than she could bear, and, hearing it, Nell silently abandoned one of the conditions she'd laid down for coming to the villa.

'I'll help as often as you like,' she said gently, 'provided you call me Nell, not Eleanor, and let me give you a little Italian lesson every morning. The people here won't mind at all if you get something wrong; they'll just be happy to know you're trying to talk to them.'

A shy smile accepted the suggestion, but they were interrupted by the arrival in the room of Sir Frank and his French guests – one of them very dapper in pale-fawn suiting, with a gold chain glinting under the open collar of his cream silk shirt; the other sheathed in a black dress so simple and so right that it could only have been cut by a master hand. In the process of being introduced, Nell was obliged to admire them both and to face what she must confess to Giles afterwards: if the fashion bar was going to be set this high, both she and Joan Middleton weren't even in the race; England's hopes would have to rest on Jacqueline.

The girl herself came into the room a moment later, not apologetic for her late arrival but confident that youth and beauty would be sufficient excuse for behaving as she pleased. A miniskirted tunic of orange silk might resemble the tabard of a medieval page, but there was nothing boyish about her provocative face and perfectly formed body; Jacqueline Middleton was all-female from head to toes.

Introduced as well to her, Nell privately marvelled at the mysterious genetic coupling that had allowed the Middletons to produce this changeling child. But conjecture was interrupted by the appearance of the evening's last guest, who had finally remembered that he must cross the courtyard and join the people who were staying in his house.

Nell liked Vittorio Guidi on sight – liked his courtly bow over her hand, his shy smile and shabby jacket that he'd forgotten to change; but she approved most of all of the kindness with which he devoted himself to his overanxious hostess. Joan Middleton even found it possible to smile at something he said, and, for a moment, Nell saw in her face the fleeting charm that perhaps had once captivated her husband.

The evening that followed went better than expected, Nell said to Giles when they were alone again in their bedroom, but he gave most of the credit to Lucia's delicious food and their host's generous supply of fine Brunello wine.

'There was a deadly silence in the room when we rejoined you ladies after dinner,' he added. 'What was that about?'

Nell shook her head. 'Not deadly – respectful, we thought! Madame de la Tour had just given us the successful woman's formula for elegance at all times: keep to one colour only for daylight hours – so much simpler that way. That colour can vary from season to season, but only black is permissible for evenings at any time of the year. She said this with her sweetest smile to the other three women there who couldn't produce a shred of black between them.'

'I told you that she was very French,' Giles commented with a grin. 'But there's no doubting her success or – if I'm allowed to mention it – her elegance! Even Frank, who is normally unimpressed by worldly women, seems rather taken with her, and, Nell, admit it: he'd have to be blind not to see the contrast with his wife.'

'Admitted freely,' she conceded; 'but our charming, absent-minded poet isn't blind either, and he knew which of them he'd rather talk to. He and Joan Middleton were getting on like a house on fire.'

Giles didn't answer until he'd stripped off his shirt and emerged from it smiling.

'It seems to leave you, dear Nell, with the task of enchanting Bertrand de la Tour! Jacqueline is much too young for him.'

It also seemed to leave the too-young Jacqueline to Giles himself, his wife noticed. She was tempted to make a joke of it – would certainly have done in the past – but a faintly proprietorial note in his voice warned her that care was needed now. Even a year ago, it wouldn't have seemed possible that their happiness was likely to be threatened; however these things were arranged, it had surely been intended that they should find and recognize each other. But recent months, spent more apart than together and largely devoted to the interests of a man she couldn't trust or like, had made a difference to them.

She was still thinking about it when he returned from the bathroom, kissed her good night, and got into one of the twin beds that he would once have objected to but now didn't even seem to notice. He was about to turn out his bedside lamp when her voice halted him.

'You haven't asked about Jonathan, but I expect you'll be glad to know that it wasn't a bad fracture – nothing that won't mend completely in time.'

There was a little silence in the room before Giles answered her. 'I'm sorry, Nell . . . I should have asked. Too many other things on my mind, I'm afraid, but that's no excuse, of course. Sleep well – it's been a long day, and even longer for you than for me. Sunday tomorrow, thank God; we'll think of something nice to do.'

She agreed and said goodnight. But tired though she was, her mind continued to worry at problems she couldn't solve. She didn't even know why they were there at all, except for Giles's vague reference to a plan for a proposed holiday complex. If he couldn't trust her with more information than that, presumably he suspected that she would disapprove of it and say so to a man he reckoned only just below Almighty God in the scheme of things. If she were to disapprove of it strongly enough to go home, it would mean, she now felt sure, the end of their marriage, but she no longer knew whether he would even care.

It wasn't just absorption in work that he found fascinating; there was someone else to be reckoned with, and Giles's silence on the subject of Jacqueline Middleton was more worrying than all his other omissions. The girl was redoubtable, he'd said, implying that she shared her father's intelligence and drive; there'd been no mention at all of a sexual appeal so blatant that it had even blinded him to the different appearance of his wife, and this was a lawyer, trained to observe details with the persistence of a hunting terrier.

Nell's tired mind regretted the holiday they'd planned to take together. By themselves, they might have been able to make up the ground they'd lost. But instinct said that mind was wrong: they'd reached a turning point that had been waiting for them all along, and it somehow came as no surprise that Tuscany should turn out to be where their future was to be settled. Her grand-mother, Nell knew, wouldn't have found it anything to marvel at. Devout Catholic though she was, Francesca had been steeped from childhood in the myths and legends of the ancient Etruscan place, where folk memory went back much further than upstart Roman times. Nonna would have said the past was never done with; life was continuous, and the future would be decided by whatever happened now.

Nell slept fitfully at last, but was woken, as dawn light filtered into the room, by a sound she hadn't expected to hear in Italy – the reedy, two-tone note of the *coculo* calling from a tree outside. It lured her to the window and a magical view: the veils of opalescent mist that floated about the garden were dissolving even as she watched the sun rising above the rim of the hills across the valley. It promised a fine, hot day, but for the moment the morning air smelled cool and sweet, and she wanted to be out in it, listening to the cuckoo in the garden. She showered and dressed quickly, left a butterfly kiss on Giles's sleeping face, and went downstairs.

Early as it was, Beppe was already there, sweeping up the damp sawdust he'd sprinkled on the floor of the hall – the time-honoured Italian way of cleaning marble.

'*Buon giorno, Signora – fa bellissimo tempo stamane.*' He said it with pride, as if he'd been personally responsible for the fine weather and now brought it to her as a gift. '*Lei vorrebbe del caffe?*'

Nell nodded and smiled her thanks but, so as not to interrupt his work, asked to be allowed to drink it in the kitchen with Lucia. He was enchanted with this idea and laid down his broom anyway in order to lead her to the large room where his wife was rolling out the day's supply of pasta. Compliments exchanged and the coffee drunk, Nell was free to let herself out into the garden's early morning peace. She rambled about, stopping here and there to smell a rose or brush her hand against a pungent herb. Then, beyond the point that she and Giles had reached the previous evening, she came across another statue almost submerged in greenery. With its coating of ivy pulled away, she found herself having to smile back at the impish, laughing face of a small boy astride his stone dolphin.

'I'd almost forgotten he was here,' said a quiet voice, and she spun round to see his owner on the path behind her.

'Count, good morning . . . am I trespassing?' she asked quickly. 'Is this your private garden?'

He shook his head, surprised to find that he hadn't wanted to walk away and avoid this gentle-voiced English girl. 'My name is Vittorio, and you are welcome to walk wherever you please.' He came to stand beside her and pat the little statue's face. 'I used to talk to him when I was a child. It didn't matter that he never talked back – he listened, and that was enough!'

Nell smiled at the picture her companion had conjured up, but heard the echo of an old sadness in his voice. 'I guess that there were no brothers or sisters to listen instead,' she suggested tentatively.

'None,' he agreed. 'My father was injured as a young man during the war – hurt in spirit, I think, not only physically. He married afterwards, but was never happy or really well, and it was my grandfather who tried to keep the estate going, even into old age. My mother left us when I was still a child; she was beautiful, I remember, but not suited to a rural life, or my father's ill health.'

It explained a lot, Nell thought, about this gentle, self-contained man; especially, perhaps, why he hadn't married. He'd grown too accustomed to loneliness to feel the usual human need for companionship.

Not daring to offer sympathy, she thought of another question instead. 'You speak English rather better than most of us do – how did that come about?'

'After I graduated from Bologna University, I spent a year at Oxford. It was the happiest time of my life. I would have liked to stay, but by then my grandfather was dead and my father was failing; I had to come home.'

Suddenly, the Count's shy smile appeared. 'I don't normally talk so much about myself – never, in fact. You are like my little stone friend here, a good listener, but *you* can talk as well! Beppe says you speak Italian; the English who flock to Tuscany rarely do.'

Nell admitted to an Italian grandmother. 'My father is a diplomat, posted to our Embassy in Moscow at the moment, but Nonna spent all her married life in London, so, in my parents' frequent absence, she brought me and my brother up. She died three years ago, but we still miss her very much.'

It was all she wanted to say about Francesca; nor did she feel justified in asking Vittorio Guidi about the likely future of his estate. Instead, she glanced at her watch and gave a rueful smile. 'I've been out here longer than I thought. I left my husband asleep, but he'll be wondering where I am by now.' Then, on the point of walking away, she added something more. 'This is a lovely place. I know that sometimes things have to change, but, even at my age, I find myself wanting to put the clock back, not forward!'

He lifted his hand in a little farewell salute but didn't answer. She'd been gentle and discreet, but he understood her underlying opinion: she didn't like Middleton's scheme and she would be disappointed if he, *il Conte*, betrayed his grandfather by allowing it to go ahead.

'She knows nothing about it,' he said to his little stone friend. 'The English – and English women especially – still can't resist telling the rest of us what we should do.'

Then, ashamed of this statement, he retracted it. 'It's not true of Signora Fanshawe, you know – she's charming and kind. But I'm afraid she's going to discover that time only moves in the direction she doesn't like.' He gave a little sigh as he walked away, regretful as much for a past he couldn't reclaim as for a future he could see no way of holding back.

Breakfast was in progress when Nell got back to the house, and the day ahead was being mapped out. Bertrand needed to be given a tour of the area, in order to acquaint himself, he said, with the shape of the landscape. Sylvie, limiting her *prima colazione* to grapefruit and black coffee, firmly declined to join him. It was *le dimanche*, after all, designated a day of rest, and she intended to spend it in a comfortable chair by the pool.

Nell waited for what might come next. If Giles really meant to put his client's interests aside for this one day, then surely not even Frank Middleton could insist otherwise. But she'd under-rated his daughter. With a sweet smile for their French guest, Jacqueline announced that, *dimanche* or not, she was prepared to do whatever driving was required.

'Giles can't explain things to Bertrand and drive at the same time,' she insisted, 'and he's the only one of us who knows the layout of this place. So I'll drive, Bertrand can ask questions, and all Giles has to do is answer them.'

'Sounds good to me,' her father said, smiling broadly at her. 'But you'll have to leave me here, sweetheart. I've a heap of papers to read, and not even those fool doctors said I mustn't do that.'

Nell looked across the table at Giles. She wanted more than anything for him to refuse politely what was being arranged for him, but habitual fairness of mind told her that he'd been driven into a corner from which there was no escape.

'Nell and I . . . we . . . we'd thought of taking a drive ourselves,' he finally muttered. Then his eyes met hers. 'You haven't seen anything of Tuscany yet – come with us, won't you?'

She shook her head and smiled at the remaining person present who hadn't so far been consulted. 'Lady Middleton and I have work of our own to do here.' It wasn't even difficult to sound cheerful. If she died in the attempt, she'd refuse Jacqueline the pleasure of thinking she minded how Giles's day was to be spent.

With breakfast over, she was tidying their bedroom when Giles came in.

'Don't apologize,' she said at once. 'Your charming boss made it clear at the airport that we were here to be useful, so we must either stay on his terms or leave. I'd be very happy to go if it weren't for his wife – she needs help.'

Relieved to be sidetracked, Giles managed a faint smile. 'Don't make a martyr of her, Nell. She didn't have to marry Frank; she chose the life she's got now – rather a comfortable one, I could point out! Let's forget about her, though. I am sorry about today, but . . .' Unable to think what else to say about it, he tried another tack. 'It *is* a lovely place. Can you make do with that – please? I know the de la Tours aren't exactly the sort of people you'd choose to spend time with but—'

This time Nell interrupted him. 'Say no more – they're an education, the pair of them!' She decided not to add that a promising battle between Sylvie and Jacqueline would also be worth watching, and Giles's expression relaxed at the note of amusement in her voice.

'I think I'd rather say that if we can at least find this rum party entertaining, we'll be managing quite well!' His smile shone for a moment as he looked at her. 'I'd better go – the others will be waiting; but don't forget I love you.'

'I won't,' she promised seriously and waved him on his way.

She waited at the window to see them drive off and then went downstairs to summon Joan Middleton to her Italian lesson. They both enjoyed the hour that followed. Nell, especially, relished having a pupil who was not only anxious to learn but also happened to have the essential requirement for getting to grips with another language – an 'ear' for the different sounds she was being asked to make.

When the lesson was over and they were drinking coffee on the terrace, Joan suddenly remembered her other guest. 'Should I see if Sylvie needs anything?'

Nell shook her head. 'Whatever she wants Madame de la Tour will ask for, I'm sure.'

'She drains what little self-confidence I have,' Nell's companion suddenly confessed. 'I can see her making a mental note of everything that's wrong about me!' Joan Middleton hesitated for a moment and then went on. 'I suppose this is something else I shouldn't say, but I can't not warn you about Jacqueline. She's used to getting everything she wants, and if it's something that seems to be out of reach, that only makes her more determined than ever.'

Unwilling to put a name to what Jacqueline might now be wanting, Nell took refuge in a generality. 'You know your own daughter, so I shall heed the warning!'

She wasn't prepared for what came next. 'I've had twenty years in which to get to know her,' said Joan Middleton, 'but she's not my daughter. Her mother – Frank's first wife – left him when Jacqueline was a year old. My ailing parents had recently died, and I answered an advertisement for a nanny-cum-housekeeper. Six months later he asked me to marry him. I knew he didn't love me, but I thought he might grow fond enough of me for us to be happy together.'

Hurt by the sadness in her voice, Nell framed a hesitant question. 'What went wrong?'

'Frank wanted more children, of course. I did get pregnant but I was unwell all the time, and very ill when our son was born. He died two days later, and I could have no more children. After that, all Frank's affection was given to Jacqueline.' She saw the expression on Nell's face and shook her head.

'I know you don't like him, but he's not a bad man. He's a fighter, but he fights fairly, and he rewards loyalty as freely as he punishes anyone who lets him down. Giles won't come to any harm from him.'

'What happened to Jacqueline's mother?' Nell asked. 'Do they know one another?'

Joan shook her head. 'Frank divorced her, of course. If she'd guessed how successful he'd become, I suppose she wouldn't have left. But she was even more beautiful than her daughter, apparently, and life in Huddersfield wasn't nearly exciting enough. Jacqueline knows about her, but she likes things the way they are: she's inherited her mother's looks but her father's brain, and he's very proud of her; they don't need anyone else now.'

Unable to ask why this defeated woman had stayed, to be ignored by her husband and despised by his daughter, Nell reverted to the way the conversation had begun.

'You mustn't let Sylvie demoralize you. I know she's the last word in chic, and much given to pitying any woman not born a Parisienne, but we're not obliged to agree with her!'

'You don't have to,' Joan agreed rather sadly, 'but it's different for me.' Then her rare smile flickered for a moment. 'When Frank said that you'd be coming with Giles, my heart sank – I remembered meeting you once in London – someone else here, I thought, to pity or patronize me. But you're kindness itself, and, as long as you stay with us, I can even survive the heat and the not understanding and the feeling that I'm completely out of place.'

Nell barely hesitated and plunged before giving herself time to think. 'The language isn't the only hurdle we could do something about. The temperature will get much higher than it is now, but you probably came kitted out for a Huddersfield summer. Why don't we go into Florence and look for the sort of simple, cool clothes that Italian women wear? You'll feel different about being here if you aren't uncomfortably hot.' While Joan thought about this, she plunged still further. 'You have lovely hair, but if you'd agree to have it cut, at least for the summer, that would help, too.'

Her companion's hands touched the heavy coil at the nape of her neck, a style she hadn't changed for twenty years. 'I suppose I could,' she said doubtfully. 'I don't know . . . yes, why not? Nell, I will, but you'll have to do the talking for me.'

'We'll go tomorrow,' said her adviser, determined to strike while the iron was still, if not hot, at least lukewarm, . 'If Beppe isn't free, there must be a bus we can take.'

'We shan't know where to go,' Joan objected anxiously.

'Yes, we shall – Via Tornabuoni is where the very best shops are. We might need to spend quite a lot of money; will your husband mind that?'

Joan's smile reappeared. 'Not if the results are worth it,' she said with rare confidence. 'He's not a Yorkshireman for nothing – he never begrudges money well spent!'

At this opportune moment Beppe came out to collect their coffee cups and lay the table for lunch. When Nell raised the possibility of a trip to Florence, he smiled benignly. *Il Signor Conte* would expect him to do whatever the English ladies wished. So it was arranged easily enough; to *la città* they would go the following morning.

# Four

At lunchtime the travellers hadn't returned, so only the remaining members of the party sat down at the terrace table as Lucia served them the pasta without which, summer or winter, no Italian meal could start. In the face of her obvious pleasure at giving these ill-nourished northerners the food they needed, not even Sylvie tried to suggest that she would forego the first course. Instead, she devoted herself to the entertainment of her host.

Both she and he knew a good deal about the ruling elite in Brussels, and neither of them appeared to notice that their conversation effectively excluded the other two people at the table. Joan Middleton was accustomed, Nell supposed, to being left out, and she made no effort to intervene herself until Sylvie attacked *l'Angleterre* for its stupid attitude towards the European Union.

'That's how it's been since the beginning,' she declared. 'Look how long it took you to decide to be part of Europe at all.'

'It's not quite how it *was*,' Nell suddenly insisted. 'Our entry at the beginning was vetoed by your anti-Anglo-Saxon President, Charles de Gaulle! An act of base ingratitude considering how he was made welcome in London in 1940 when France collapsed.' Then, sweetly, she smiled at her opponent. 'But it's true that a lot of people on our side of the Channel think we do better when we're on our own – it comes of living on an island, I'm afraid.'

'A very small island,' Sylvie was glad to point out, before abandoning European history for a subject she knew more about.

With lunch finally over, Nell considered the outlook for the rest of the afternoon. Joan Middleton would seize the excuse of a siesta and escape; her husband would return to his paperwork. It left a tête-à-tête with Sylvie or the good, health-giving walk that the English were known to be addicted to. She announced firmly that she would visit Poggione; it was Sunday and she hadn't been to Mass, but she could at least call in at the church. No one challenged this strange ambition and she was free to set off

alone. The fierce summer heat was still to come, so for the moment
the roadside was bordered by a flood of wild flowers. The brilliant Tuscan anemones made pools of colour everywhere, and
there were many other flowers she couldn't even put a name to.

When she reached Poggione, the little town seemed to be fast
asleep, but the doors of the church were open and she walked
inside, grateful for its cool, incense-scented darkness after the glare
outside. She knelt to pray – for Giles, her parents and Jonathan
– and to remember her grandmother, whose loss still made her
want to weep. On her feet again, she lit a candle for Francesca
and then went slowly back to the door.

Next to it was something she hadn't noticed on the way in:
a stone tablet let into the wall, inscribed with a list of names and a
number beside each one. The notice underneath explained that
it commemorated the young boys who had been shot in 1944
by the German occupying troops – a reprisal against partisan
resistance. Halfway down the list was a name that made Nell's
heartbeat falter – Franco Pizzoni, who had been killed at the age
of fifteen.

Too shocked to move, she wasn't even aware of no longer
being alone; then a voice behind her asked if she was a visitor
to Poggione. She turned to see the priest standing there, took a
deep breath and managed to answer him. Yes, she agreed, she was
a visitor staying at the Villa Guidi. Then she pointed to the tablet.

'Francesca Pizzoni was my grandmother. I knew she had a
younger brother, but she never explained that he was killed, or
even said where in Tuscany her family lived. Can you tell me,
please, what happened?'

'Only at second-hand, I'm afraid, Signora. You should hear the
story from my father – he was a child here at the time. He's
sitting outside in the cloister.'

Led through the vestry door, she found herself shaking hands
with a frail, white-haired man, introduced to her as Luciano
Pavese. His son explained why she was there and then left them
alone together. Asked to look back nearly sixty years, the old man
had no difficulty in recalling a scene that had never faded from
his mind.

'The Germans were getting desperately short of men by then,
you must understand,' he began quietly. 'But our young men had

gone into hiding in the mountains and joined the partisans instead. One day a German convoy was ambushed – soldiers were killed and a lot of weapons stolen. The people here were asked to betray the partisans' hiding place, and when they refused, their children were taken instead and shot. It was the worst thing that happened in all those terrible years.' Then Signor Pavese stared more closely at Nell. 'How did Francesca come to be your grandmother?'

Nell told him the brief story, then hesitated over what to say next. 'She never came back here after her marriage, and the letters she wrote to her father were returned unopened – I only found them after she died. I never discovered from her what went wrong, but now, knowing about Franco, I can understand: Luigi Pizzoni needed her to marry an Italian, not a man who would take her away from Tuscany.'

A reminiscent smile touched the old man's face. 'I can remember her still – such a very lovely girl she was. No wonder the Englishman came back for her after the war, but she should have stayed here where everybody loved her.'

'We loved her too,' Nell insisted. Then she frowned over her next question. 'Franco died here in Poggione, but Francesca's letters were addressed to a place called Pratolino – is that nearby?'

'Yes, down in the valley,' he said vaguely, then went on to answer the next question in her mind. 'I left to become a school-teacher and for many years didn't live here at all, but I'm sure there's no one by the name of Pizzoni living in the valley now – in fact, most of the farms are lying idle.'

'So it's true, then,' Nell said. 'People have left the land to find easier work in the cities.'

He nodded his white head. 'But it wasn't only the work, you understand. They wanted to escape the system as well; *mezzadria*, it was called. The landowner supplied the farm, the equipment and stock; the tenant paid no rent, but received no wage, and gave half of what he produced to the owner. It went on like that for centuries, even after the war ended, but nowadays people want money to spend, and money was something the tenants scarcely ever had.'

He fell silent for a moment, then asked a question of his own. 'My son mentioned the villa: so you know the present Count?'

'My husband and I have met him,' Nell said, 'but we're staying with some other people in part of the house that he rents out.'

'Not quite how things were,' her companion pointed out. 'The Guidis owned much of this part of Tuscany even in the old Count's time – this man's grandfather, I mean. I can remember him well, riding about on a huge horse, telling us what to do, laying down Guidi law! Life was still medieval, so, of course, things had to change, but I'm afraid they've changed far too quickly.'

Warned by the tiredness in his voice, Nell knew that it was time to leave. She thanked him for talking to her and got up, holding out her hand. He bent his head over it in a charming gesture and hoped that she would visit him again. She promised that she would and then, following the direction he indicated, found that a small door at the far end of the cloister took her out into the lane that led back to the piazza.

The return journey to the villa had to be viewed differently now. Francesca had grown up in this very part of Tuscany, had probably walked this road to school every day and to Mass on Sundays. And it was in the piazza Nell had just left behind that a young boy and his friends had been herded together and shot according to the brutal realities of total warfare.

Only Beppe was visible when she reached the villa. After listening to a kindly lecture on the rashness of a long walk in the heat of the day, she was allowed to escape to her bedroom. Half an hour later when Giles walked in, she was sketching the view from the window.

'Welcome back,' she said, smiling at him. 'You look even hotter than I felt after my walk. Was it a day well spent, though?'

'I suppose so,' he agreed grudgingly. 'I was hoping to come back at lunchtime, but Bertrand would have had us still out there if Jacqueline hadn't refused to drive any further.' Nell looked sympathetic and was rewarded with an apologetic smile. 'A boring day for you, my poor girl – I'm sorry.'

'Don't be,' she said. 'Lunch was enlivened by a stimulating little brush with dear Sylvie – whom, I tell you now, I shall never grow to like! Then this afternoon something very different happened. It's a long story, so I'll wait until you've showered to tell you about it.'

When he reappeared a quarter of an hour later, he didn't look impatient to hear what she had to say, but her serious face seemed to suggest that it might be important after all. She recounted her visit to the church and her conversation with the priest's father in a voice that broke in the telling. There was a long pause before Giles himself found something to say.

'Why did Francesca never talk about it?' he asked finally.

'I've been thinking about that – I suppose because she felt guilty about leaving her father,' Nell could only suggest. 'Grandfather wasn't here in 1944, by the way – he'd left by then to walk south and join up with the British Army fighting its way up Italy.'

Giles nodded but asked another question. 'Poggione is central to what happened, but that isn't the name you mentioned, is it – the address on Francesca's letters?'

'It was a place called Pratolino, but Signor Pavese said it was nearby – down in the valley. Most of the land is lying idle now, apparently, so I can't help thinking that it's exactly what Frank Middleton is hoping to buy from the Count.'

Giles had still another question. 'Did your old man know what had happened to the Pizzonis?'

Nell shook her head. 'He'd been away for years, working as a schoolteacher. But he seemed quite certain that no one of that name is living here now. His son, as the local priest, would surely know.'

Giles pulled a wry face. 'Just as well perhaps! Having a descendant of Francesca's here in the middle of our negotiations might have done us no good at all! We won't mention it to Frank, Nell – however extraordinary it is to us, it's not relevant to his affairs.' He was silent for a moment, then smiled at her. 'I can guess what you're thinking: our visit here was meant to happen! Am I right?'

She nodded, agreeing more seriously than he had asked the question. 'I've had an odd feeling about it ever since we got here. It's almost a relief to know there's a reason for it.' She put her sketchbook aside and stood up. 'You've been cooped up in a car all day – how about a walk?'

'More than anything, I'd like a swim.' Then, more hesitantly, he went on. 'I must keep my appointment with the lawyers in Florence tomorrow. Frank wants Jacqueline there as well. She won't add anything to the meeting except a little glamour which the Italians will like, but she's hungry to learn all she can.'

Nell considered this for a moment and then nodded. 'Yes, that's the word for her – hungry,' she agreed matter-of-factly.

But Giles understood what had been left unsaid. 'She's concerned for her father,' he said sharply; 'wants to be all the help she can. It seems admirable to me.'

Nell longed to point out that for once he wasn't being honest; deliberately or unconsciously, he was blinding himself to what they were really arguing about. It was so unlike him that she was made more sharply aware of the threat that Jacqueline Middleton represented. She also found herself wondering whether he knew about the girl's mother. He'd become so intimate with them that it was hard to believe he wasn't in the secret, in which case it was something else he'd chosen not to share with her.

Nell abruptly changed the subject. 'Joan Middleton and I are also going in to Florence tomorrow – Beppe is taking us.'

'Doing the sights?' Giles asked in a more friendly voice.

'They'll come later; some serious shopping is on the agenda first. Huddersfield clothes are not what are needed here.' She might have left it at that, but his known view of Joan Middleton made her go on. 'Feeling more comfortable will help her get through this summer, but she'll need more than that. I'm going to enrol Count Guidi in my "save Joan" campaign – I think it will be good for both of them.'

Giles looked disapproving again. 'Meddling in other people's lives, Nell? I thought you didn't agree with that.'

'Someone has to help her,' Nell answered simply, 'and it might as well be me.'

Giles studied his wife in silence for a moment, still trying to pin down the alteration in her that eluded him. Whatever the reason, she wasn't the same woman who had got ready under protest a week ago to come with him to Tuscany.

'You've changed,' he said almost accusingly. 'It isn't just that you can understand what goes on here and the rest of us can't; it goes deeper than that. This visit is important to you in ways I haven't fathomed out yet, but the legal brain is working on it!'

'I think it's important to both of us,' she agreed seriously, 'but while you're thinking about it, why not go and have that swim?

I've had a long walk this afternoon so I shall do no more than·
sprawl in a poolside chair. But I'll cheer you on if Sylvie and
Jacqueline aren't there to provide the admiring chorus!'

'And I, dear Nell, might just push you into the water.'

Her smile acknowledged that she might have goaded him too
far, and, with a kind of peace restored, she followed him downstairs. Sylvie was nowhere to be seen, but Jacqueline was already
there, less chastely draped than the stone maidens who watched
over the pool. Her smile inviting Giles to dive in after her told
Nell that even this shared swim had been prearranged between
them.

Rather than stay and look on, she did what the young Vittorio
had done long ago and went to tell her trouble to the little
listener astride his dolphin.

# Five

The following morning Nell left it to Joan Middleton to explain to her husband that they would be absent for most of the day. Her own preparations were to warn Lucia not to expect them for lunch, to consult Carlotta about hairdressing establishments, and then to study the city's street map. After that they were ready to set off.

She feared that her protégée's nerve might be weakening, so it seemed prudent to make a salon their first port of call. When Beppe had deposited them outside the General Post Office and left with instructions to collect them again at half past three, she led her lamb towards Carlotta's recommended *parrucchiere* for the slaughter.

Their unexpected arrival seemed not to matter at all; of course, the signora could be attended to, *subito!* Her need was explained by Nell, who saw an answering gleam in the eye of the young man assigned to them. The hair itself was good, he pronounced – fine in the way of English hair, but still thick; the colour – fair, now frosting to silver – pretty and unusual; but the too-severe style! However, hand on heart, he promised that if the signora would leave that to him, all would be well.

Nell nervously awaited the result. Giles had been right: she was meddling without excuse in someone else's life, and although she meant well, the road to hell was proverbially paved with such intentions. But the young man was as good as his word – a smiling Joan reappeared quite soon with a charming bob and broken fringe that, as he rightly said, combined the casual and the elegant. With her teacher's eye upon her, Joan even plucked up the courage to repeat a phrase she'd learned – '*Mi piace molto . . . mille grazie!*' – and they were shown out on a fine exchange of mutual good wishes.

'Now where?' she asked. 'That *via* you mentioned?' She even sounded different, Nell thought, ready for whatever adventure she was offered next.

'Not Tornabuoni, after all. I asked the receptionist at the salon, who said not unless we had the nerve to stroll into Armani or Dolce & Gabbana and ask for something off the peg! But in Via dei Calzaiuoli – in the street of the shoemakers – there's a department store where we can get everything you need at a fraction of the price. If my street map doesn't lie, the street we're in now will lead us straight to it.'

They found it easily enough, and spent a happy couple of hours raiding it for simple linen and silk dresses, cotton skirts, and shirts in the shades that suited Joan's delicate colouring – cream, apricot, turquoise and pale-green. Then, heavily laden, they made for the nearest trattoria and settled themselves at one of its pavement tables.

'Just time for lunch before we stagger back to meet Beppe again,' said Nell. 'What fun it's been – at least I hope you think so?'

Joan waited while a hovering waiter took Nell's order – bruschetta topped with prosciutto and *melone*, and a flask of local white wine. By the time he left them alone, she'd found what she wanted to say. 'More fun than I've ever known before. Now I know what I've missed, not having a daughter. Thank you, dear Nell.' Her mouth trembled for a moment, but she managed a grateful smile instead.

To ease the emotional moment, Nell began to speak of the treasures all around them, barely skimmed by the visiting hordes that came to 'do' Florence in a week or a fortnight. 'A lifetime here wouldn't exhaust all there is to see,' she said wistfully, 'and that's before you start on Venice or Rome; not to mention every small Italian town that has something gorgeous and rare hidden away.'

'At least you'd know what to look for,' Joan pointed out with a trace of sadness in her voice. 'An upbringing in Northumberland didn't prepare me for all this; although it did teach me to love landscapes and made it hard for me to accept life in Huddersfield at first. Yorkshire can be wild and beautiful, of course, but it's different here – it's been made beautiful by the people who've worked it – shaped it, I suppose Bertrand would say!'

Noting the mischievous smile that came with that last comment, Nell realized that the morning had done wonders for her companion. At this rate of progress, there was no telling what

might happen next. She could even begin to cope with her overbearing husband and contemptuous stepdaughter. But, as if she'd
just added mind-reading to her new possibilities, she now spoke
of those people herself.

'I know why you've gone to so much trouble for me, Nell,
and I shall manage better because of it, but you mustn't expect
any great change in the way we live. In Frank's view, I *did* let
him down by not producing the sons he wanted to carry on all
his enterprises. I couldn't even carry off the sort of lifestyle they
earned – I'd been the daughter of a country parson! Once
Jacqueline was reared safely, my usefulness was over.'

'But you stayed all the same,' Nell pointed out gently. 'Why,
when you could have a happier life somewhere else?'

Joan thought about this as if it was a question she'd never asked
herself. 'I suppose because even *my* leaving would have been
another wound to Frank's pride, and his first wife had hurt him
too much already. If he ever wanted a divorce, of course I'd agree,
but I'd like him to be the one to ask. Does that sound very stupid
and spineless?'

Nell shook her head. 'Quite the contrary – it sounds more
generous than he deserves. But I agree with you about not being
the one to break up a relationship; you have to keep hoping that
it will survive.' Then, afraid of having given too much away about
herself and Giles, she signalled to the waiter for their bill and
said it was time to go in search of Beppe.

When they arrived back at the villa, there were sounds of
activity in the kitchen quarters, but there was no one to be seen
until Carlotta emerged to say that the French signori had gone
to Arezzo; the others she didn't know about, except that they'd
gone out together and everyone would be back in time for dinner.

Bertrand and Sylvie were the first to reappear in the *salone*,
where Joan and Nell waited for them. They observed, of course,
the change in the appearance of their hostess, and acknowledged
it with a nicely judged mixture of surprise and praise. Giles, who
came in next, went so far as to pat her on the back – high praise,
Nell pointed out. The final hurdle was the one that mattered
most, and she found that she was holding her breath when Frank
Middleton and his daughter arrived. He stopped dead at the sight
of his wife.

'Good God, it's Joan!' Further inspection led him to say that he'd have to get used to it, but it was certainly an improvement.

Jacqueline seemed to concentrate on her stepmother's elegantly simple silk dress. Nell watched her, thinking that if the girl dared to murmur something about mutton dressed as lamb, she, Nell Fanshawe, would have to be forcibly restrained from killing her. But, perhaps scenting danger, Jacqueline contented herself with a faintly lifted eyebrow, and then announced that the Count would be joining them for dinner again.

'I met him outside,' she explained airily. 'It seemed stupid for Lucia to be trundling food round the house to him when he could eat it here. In any case, we're a man short at the dinner table.'

It mattered not, Nell thought, to this egocentric force of nature that even if Vittorio Guidi preferred to eat alone, he would be too courteous to say so. Even less would she care that it was for her stepmother to issue invitations to her dinner table.

But it was true that the atmosphere in the room lightened when Beppe ushered the Count in a moment later. He offered them a general bow, but went to greet his hostess. Her altered appearance wasn't commented upon, but his shy smile said that he'd noticed it, and it was all the acknowledgment she needed, Nell reckoned.

Formality was dispensed with this evening; they all returned together to the *salone* when dinner was over, and Sylvie launched herself on a comparison of French and Italian cuisine – the one very '*haute*', of course, the other the '*cucina povera*', which, in her view, consisted of bread, garlic, olive oil, and very little else.

Hoping that it was someone else's turn to argue with her, Nell was grateful to the Count for pointing out the obvious: their 'poor' cuisine had been a necessity for a poor country. Things were different now, but it still relied on wonderful local ingredients and the loving care that Italy's peasant cooks bestowed on them.

All well and good, said Frank Middleton, always ready to engage in battle, but Sylvie had been talking about subtlety and finesse, about cooking raised to a high art, not farmhouse fare. The Count – no doubt remembering that these people were to some extent his guests – was prepared to yield with grace, but it was Bertrand who now stepped bravely into the firing line.

'This isn't fair, *ma chère*,' he said to his wife. 'You cannot compare what renowned Parisian chefs produce with the daily meals that hard-working cooks like Lucia must provide. But, speaking for myself, there was no finesse lacking in the wild mushroom lasagne she gave us this evening!'

Sylvie gave a little shrug, and, even more unexpectedly, it was Joan Middleton who now took the conversation in hand.

'Bertrand has rightly spoken up for Lucia, who does indeed offer us delicious meals, but I should like Count Vittorio to know as well how beautifully Beppe looks after us – he is such a kind and helpful man.'

'Even kind enough to pretend that my Italian conversation is progressing by leaps and bounds,' Giles put in with a smile. 'We both know it isn't true!'

'They are good people,' the Count agreed seriously, 'as are their children – Carlotta, and Gianni who runs the farm for me. I'm fortunate that they want to stay. Most young people find city life more attractive. Is that not true, Signorina?' he asked, turning to Jacqueline.

'Of course it's true,' she answered at once. 'Who wants to go back to how things used to be?'

He smiled across the room at Nell, reminding her of their conversation in the garden the previous morning, and then it was her turn to ask a question.

'When I talked to the priest's father in Poggione, he said that it was the system people wanted to escape from – *mezzadria*, he called it. Does it still exist?'

'I have one remaining tenant, but take nothing from him,' the Count said. 'Generally speaking, our people now own the land they farm, as indeed they should.' Then, obviously feeling that he'd been sociable enough, he thanked the Middletons for their hospitality and said goodnight. It left those who wanted to play bridge free to do so, and allowed Nell and Joan Middleton to plead tiredness after a day's shopping and go to bed.

Nell, in dressing gown and slippers, was writing when Giles finally walked in.

'I thought you'd be asleep by now,' he commented. 'You did say you were tired.'

'I was tired of being where I was,' she answered honestly;

'among the people I was with.' Then she closed the notebook she'd been writing in. 'How did you get on this morning?'

'Well enough, I suppose, considering the tortuousness of the Italian legal system. I thought ours was bad enough, but it's simplicity itself compared with what goes on here. However, Frank is now the owner of one of the valley farms, and acquiring the one next to it is a mere formality – the man is anxious to give up and retire to Arezzo. That leaves one still tenanted – the Count spoke of it this evening – but the farmer is elderly, and his children no longer live here. Once we've agreed terms with him, Frank can go ahead.'

'With what?' Nell asked baldly. 'Or is his great scheme still to be shrouded in mystery?'

'There's no mystery about it – he dreams of building the most beautiful hotel in the world, and Bertrand, for all his finicky ways, is capable of designing it. What *he* does on the outside, Sylvie will match on the inside. I've no idea how successful their marriage is, but as a design team there's no one to match them.' Then Giles registered the expression on Nell's face. 'You still don't like the idea?'

'I hate it,' she said frankly. 'These clever people are going to waste some of Italy's most fertile land on a hotel that only its wealthiest visitors can hope to afford.' She lifted her hand, asking Giles to allow her to go on before he objected to what she had said. 'My dear, we live on an overpopulated planet where millions of people have to go hungry. Food can be grown here more abundantly than almost anywhere else. That's what is needed, not yet another luxurious playground for oil-rich Arabs and Russian oligarchs.'

She expected Giles to be angry, but instead he came to squat down beside her and take hold of her hand. 'Darling Nell, you're right in theory, of course. In practice, though, this fertile land is very difficult to work. It can only produce food if people are still willing to take on the back-breaking labour involved. Dislike it if you must, but Frank's hotel will produce work and income for an area that will otherwise slowly die.'

The sadness in her face acknowledged that his argument was hard to defeat, and he went on more gently still. 'It's all too much, isn't it, finding that this is the very place where Francesca grew

up. Go home if you want to, Nell. I believe that what Frank
wants to do is right, and I'm committed to helping him, but you
don't have to stay.' His fingers lightly touched the hollows beneath
her cheek bones; she'd grown thinner, surely? 'We planned to
have more time together but we seem to have even less. It's all
gone wrong somehow – I'm sorry, Nell.'

Struggling not to weep, she knew better than to point out
whose fault it was. He already thought her irrational in her dislike
of a man he saw as a heroic, self-made legend. What would he
say if she additionally accused the man's daughter of using sheer
animal sexuality as her fighting weapon? He was, for the moment
at least, in thrall to Jacqueline; Nell knew it as surely as she knew
anything, and the knowledge made a glass barrier between them
– invisible but somehow unbreakable. Just for a moment, she was
tempted to shout at him what she believed might be the truth
– that another Middleton plan was to destroy her marriage so
that Giles could be freed to provide one of them with a husband
and the other with a very useful son-in-law. But she couldn't
bring herself to put the thought into words and finally chose
something else to say instead.

'I'd rather stay. There might never be another chance to find
out for certain what kept Francesca away from Tuscany. I promised to go and see Signor Pavese again, and he may have more
locked away in his memory about her than he realizes.'

'Of course stay, then,' said Giles, 'but be prepared for what
finding out might mean – it isn't always the result you hope for.'

'I realize that,' Nell answered quietly, 'but finding out is better
than never knowing the truth,' and the tone of her voice told
him that they were now talking about themselves and not about
her grandmother.

# Six

With the morning's Italian lesson over and her pupil in the kitchen watching Lucia start on making the day's pasta, Nell was free to set out on a quest of her own. She intended to free the Count's childhood friend from the jungle that had grown up around him. It seemed a reasonable guess, given that the laughing boy's companion was a dolphin, that the two of them had once splashed happily in water. Armed with shears and secateurs borrowed from Beppe, she meant to find out whether her guess was right or not.

The day was still young and the sun not too hot, and she hacked and snipped to her heart's content, thankful to be on her own, away from a house that seemed overfilled with powerful personalities. With a mound of brambles and weeds cleared away, she had just discovered what she was looking for – the stone rim that had surely edged the dolphin's pool – when the Count spoke behind her, as he'd done once before.

'Tell me what you're doing, please, Signora Nell, apart from "annihilating all that's made to a green thought in a green shade".'

She turned to smile at him, wondering how usual it was even for an English-speaking Italian aristocrat to be able to quote from the seventeenth-century poems of Andrew Marvell.

'"Green" is a good word, and so is "annihilating"!' she agreed. 'I'm laying about me with Beppe's tools to rescue your little listener and his friend. Am I right in thinking that there used to be water here?'

Vittorio nodded. 'The pool was fed by a little spring in the hillside just above this part of the garden. It will start to fill again now.' He waved despairingly at the jungle around them. 'What must you think of this after your beautiful English gardens? Hot summers and abundant water from the hills create this . . . this exuberance, of course, but someone else would have managed better, I'm sure, to keep it under control. I'm not a very – what is the word in English? – deedy man, I'm afraid, but you will have realized that by now.'

'Deediness takes different forms,' she pointed out. 'We can't all be fanatical gardeners; you do other things . . . like write poetry. Do you write in English as well as Italian?'

He shook his head. 'I've tried, because *your* language is the one for poetry, but the rhythms and cadences are too different for a foreigner.' He spoke with the gentle melancholy that seemed natural to him, and a ladybird that had got itself upside down and needed righting absorbed him for a moment. Then his shy, sweet smile appeared. 'I stopped at the kitchen on my way out to speak to Beppe. Donna Joanna was there, laughing because he was mimicking Lucia's way of talking to herself when she's making pasta. Our English lady looked a different person – young again and happy.'

Nell hesitated over how to reply. To agree that 'happy' wasn't how Joan Middleton usually looked would lead them into discussing the awkward question of why not. But something else he'd said could be touched on. 'I shall think of her as Joanna in future – so much prettier than our version of the name.'

'I was told about the Italian lessons, and your kindness to her,' the Count commented, then he pointed to what she was doing. 'You seem to make kindness a habit.'

Nell waved that away. 'She's making rapid progress – I can promise she'll be talking confidently before the summer is out.'

'And then she will go back home – to Huddersfield,' he pointed out, becoming mournful again. 'It has a lowering sound, don't you think, "Huddersfield"?'

'Compared with Tuscany, we might have to think it a lowering sort of place,' Nell admitted with a smile. 'Industrial cities usually are. But Sir Frank wouldn't agree; the countryside isn't where exciting enterprises are carried on.' Nell heard what she'd just said and shook her head. 'He wouldn't agree with *that* either. Giles says you know about his hotel project – that must seem exciting enough to him.'

'And to you it seems hateful,' Vittorio said, taking her by surprise. 'You think I'm selling my birthright for the Bible's "mess of pottage"!'

She blushed for the accuracy of his guess and marvelled again at the knowledge he had of English literary traditions. 'It certainly seems wrong,' she admitted, 'but I understand the problems. If land isn't to be worked, it must be used for other purposes. I shall make an effort to think of Frank Middleton as a benefactor, not a barbarian.'

The Count threw back his head and laughed out loud and, just as he'd seen a different Joanna, Nell now glimpsed the young man he had been. Sober again, he touched her grubby hand. 'Thank you for caring for my friend here; I should have looked after him myself.'

'It's a labour of love,' Nell said. 'I'd rather be out of the house.'

He nodded as if he understood that and walked away, leaving her with two clear impressions: one that a couple of conversations had been enough to make them friends; and the other that he'd grown concerned about the benefactor's wife. Fellow feeling, Nell supposed, for someone else leading a lonely, unshared life.

She returned to work and had the pleasure of seeing a trickle of water already beginning to collect on the floor of the dolphin's pool which wouldn't now be swallowed up by rampant greenery. She was smiling at his small rider when the next interruption occurred, and Bertrand de la Tour came to stand beside her. It was irritating to think he'd watched her smiling at a statue, but she supposed it would simply reinforce the opinion held by most French people that the English were mad. Then irritation died, because, in his spotless cream trousers and monogrammed shirt, he looked so out of place in the lovely wilderness around them that she felt sorry for him.

'You see before you a prospector who's found gold,' she announced, smiling at him. 'The water's coming back and the dolphin will be able to swim again!'

He nodded, only half aware of what she'd said because he was suddenly so acutely aware of *her*. Had he not looked at her carefully enough before? A woman who needed that care because she made no obvious demand on a man's attention. He *was* seeing her now, with the sun painting golden glints in her brown hair and already turning her clear skin honey-coloured.

Surprised by his silence, Nell began to gather up Beppe's tools, then had them taken out of her hands. 'They're rather oily,' she said quickly. 'I can carry them.'

'So can I; and my trousers, should they get dirty, can be washed,' Bertrand pointed out. 'I was sent by Lady Middleton to find you – cooling drinks are on the terrace, and you must surely be in need of one.'

The smile he'd been waiting for touched Nell's mouth again. 'I am indeed, but I must clean myself up first.'

When they'd climbed the stone steps leading to the upper level of the garden and were side by side again, she risked a question. 'Am I allowed to ask how your plans are going, or do you not talk about them yet?'

'I'd talk about them gladly if I knew what they were.' He stood still for a moment, and she had to stop too, while he put his thought into words. 'I came to Tuscany imagining that I'd design something entirely of today – startlingly modern, but so beautiful that it would "fit" even here. All I know at the moment is that it can't be done – new, however beautiful, won't fit, not here. The sense of continuity with the past is too strong.'

Nell nodded, understanding what he meant. 'It's even visible in the people themselves. Faces in the street seem familiar, simply because they still look like every painting you've ever seen of fifteenth-century Florentines! Count Vittorio, for example, is the spitting image of Cosimo Medici.'

'The same beaky nose, and skin drawn tight across the skull and cheekbones – yes, you're right,' Bertrand agreed with sudden pleasure. 'So, to answer your question, Frank's hotel is probably going to hide inside a traditional Tuscan castle after all.'

'Well, that's something to be thankful for at least,' said Nell, starting to walk on again. 'A glass and concrete monstrosity in the depths of Tuscany simply wouldn't do.'

About to protest that nothing he designed was monstrous, the glimmer of amusement in her face made him change his mind, and then the conversation came to an end because they'd reached the terrace steps.

When Nell reappeared, clean and cool again, there was a newcomer to the party – Father Pavese from the church in Poggione. He stood up to shake hands with her and then offered her the envelope he'd brought with him.

'From my father, Signora – he is a little unwell at the moment, but he was anxious for you to have this. After your visit he searched through all his mementoes of the past and found an old photograph that he thought you would like. He wishes you to keep it.' Then, in broken English, the priest apologized to the others for speaking in Italian, and excused himself from staying longer – he had someone to visit in nearby Poppi.

Nell thanked him warmly, but there was a little silence after he'd left that she felt obliged to break.

'It's a strange coincidence,' she began hesitantly, 'but it seems that my grandmother grew up in this part of Italy. I only discovered that when I spoke to Signor Pavese and found that he had known her as a child. It was kind of him to think of sending me the photograph.'

As she spoke, she put the envelope in the pocket of her skirt, and something in her voice said that she would answer no more questions about it. Then Lucia and Carlotta appeared, carrying out the spaghetti *alla carbonara* that Joan Middleton had watched being made, and whatever little mystery attached to Nell's grandmother was forgotten by the others.

They were just beginning lunch when Giles and Jacqueline came back after another morning visit to the Count's lawyer in Florence.

'Farm number two done and dusted,' Jacqueline said carelessly, as if the business of acquiring land in Italy was almost too easy to be interesting to a girl who liked to apply her wits to beating the opposition. But, looking at Giles, Nell saw the expression on *his* face that told her something on his mind needed thinking about.

Invigorated by a morning spent hurling instructions to his staff in London by telephone and internet, Frank Middleton shared his daughter's optimism. 'So we're nearly there, then?' he asked of Giles. 'Only the Count's remaining tenant to strike a deal with.'

'Nearly there,' Giles agreed, applying himself to the plate Lucia had put in front of him. It would be soon enough when he was alone with his client to mention that something in the other lawyer's attitude had worried him. The man hadn't admitted to there being a problem, but his own professional antennae were finely tuned and he'd come away feeling that farm number three might turn out to be a possible stumbling block.

So it proved the following day when the Count's lawyer arrived at the villa. It seemed that the tenant, Sergio Ruffini, though elderly, didn't wish to give up his farm, even though his children, whose careers were in the city, had no interest in it. His grandson, Marco, *had* chosen to stay with him at Pratolino.

Frank Middleton considered this in silence for a moment before he answered. 'Ruffini has heard from his neighbour, and he's been waiting for us, of course. I don't blame him for thinking this is the time to be difficult, but I'm not a patient man and I need that land. I'll pay whatever is reasonable to get him out quickly, but I won't be taken for a fool.'

'But it isn't his land,' Giles put in. 'As I understand it, he's still the Count's tenant – he can be asked to leave.'

The Florentine lawyer looked from one to the other of them, wondering who to address his bad news to first. 'I'm afraid the real problem is that he doesn't consider himself a tenant. He believes that he was given the farm by his relative before the man died. If this is true, he can't be evicted, only negotiated with. I haven't seen it yet, but he claims to have a document giving him legal entitlement to the land.'

Then Middleton spoke again, more calmly than Giles expected. 'We shall have to interrupt whatever Count Guidi is doing at the moment.' Beppe was summoned and instructed to find his master. Five minutes later he returned with Vittorio Guidi behind him.

At a nod from his client, Giles repeated what had been said so far. 'There's been a rather serious misunderstanding somewhere along the line,' he finished up, 'but we need to get it cleared up quickly – it's on that land that Sir Frank's hotel is going to be built.'

'It's a simple question to be answered,' Middleton put in. 'Whose land *is* it – yours, Count, or Ruffini's?'

Giles winced at the inference: if the farmer was right, then Vittorio Guidi was guilty of misleading them. There was a sudden tinge of colour in the Italian's face, but he spoke with a gentle dignity that Giles secretly applauded.

'Remember, please, that I was born after the war ended. I must rely on what I learned from my father, who was a young man at the time. His father – the old Count, as people still think of him here – commanded the local partisan unit during the war. In the course of an action, his tenant's young son was killed, along with other boys. The farmer blamed my grandfather, not the Germans – the reprisal should have been expected. As some kind of compensation, the poor man was allowed to consider the farm his while he lived – no rent was to be paid, no share of his produce given to the *padrone*. That didn't change after he died – neither my father nor I subsequently made any claim on the relative who continued to live there – but legally it reverted to being Guidi land again.'

The Count's reproof was faint but unmistakable, and Frank Middleton sounded less brusque when he spoke again. 'Do you think there's any document lying around that would make that clear?'

'I shall search through what family papers I have,' said the Count, 'but please remember that we are talking about 1944 – a truly desperate time here, when the normal way of doing anything simply didn't apply.'

It was agreed that a meeting with Sergio Ruffini must await whatever the Count could find. Then Middleton thought of another question. 'What sort of relation is Ruffini to the man who died – his younger son?'

The lawyer shook his head. 'He had no other son. He brought his married sister and her family to live at the farm – Sergio grew up there.'

'So the original tenant wasn't called Ruffini at all?'

Giles waited for the lawyer's answer, knowing as surely as night followed day what it would be.

'No, it was a man called Pizzoni – Luigi Pizzoni,'

At that pregnant moment, the meeting broke up. Following the others to the door, Giles had time to school his face into indifference again before goodbyes had to be said.

Then, hotfoot, he went in search of his wife.

# Seven

Nell was finally run to earth in a secluded corner of the garden. It had obviously been someone else's chosen spot because an arbour overhung with roses sheltered a small table and a couple of chairs. She was sitting at the table writing when Giles appeared.

'You look busy, but can I interrupt? It's rather urgent, Nell,' he said half-apologetically.

She laid down her pen, accustomed to the knowledge that the creating of books for children wasn't something he took very seriously. 'I was busy,' she agreed, 'but you have interrupted, so fire away.'

He recounted what had happened – the visit of the Florentine lawyer and Count Guidi's contribution to the discussion. 'So now we know,' he finished up dolefully. 'Your unlamented great-grandfather *is* at the bottom of all this, and it's going to get unpleasant before we sort it out.'

For a moment, Nell barely took in what Giles had just said; she was more concerned with the novel idea of discovering that there were Italian relatives that she hadn't known existed. Working out the connection, she finally announced that since Ruffini's mother had been her great-grandfather's sister, it must make them cousins of a very distant sort.

'No doubt,' Giles agreed shortly, 'but it's not what we have to think about, Nell. I know I suggested not telling Frank of your connection with this place, but I think he has to be told now. The past is going to be delved into – there's no way of avoiding that – and I'd rather he heard the story from us, not accidentally from someone else.'

Nell nodded reluctantly. 'I'd much rather he didn't know, for no good reason that I can think of, but he already knows that my grandmother was born here – I had to explain that much when Father Pavese brought me his father's photograph of Francesca and Franco.'

'That settles it, then. I'll go and talk to Frank now. Will you come too, or would you rather not?' Giles asked.

'Yes, I'll come; in fact, I think I'd prefer to do the telling myself,' Nell heard herself say with some surprise.

They found Middleton in the small room that must once have been the Contessa's private sitting room, but its delicate charm had been obliterated by his aggressively male personality and the trappings of a powerful man doing business on a global scale. At the sight of Jacqueline also there, Nell hesitated in the doorway, but Giles's hand on her arm urged her forward. Feeling like an erring schoolgirl sent to own up to the head prefect, she spoke more bluntly than she meant to.

'I've come to let you know that Luigi Pizzoni was my great-grandfather,' she announced. 'Giles thinks that's something you ought to be told. My grandmother's younger brother was one of the boys shot by the Germans. Luigi Pizzoni never forgave her for leaving Tuscany after the war, but she'd fallen in love with the English prisoner of war they had sheltered, and when he went back for her she moved with him to London. Francesca must have known her aunt, but she never mentioned her or the husband and children her aunt must have had. The letters she wrote to her father from London were returned unopened.'

There was silence in the room when Nell had finished speaking, while Frank Middleton fed into his brain the information she had just given him.

'Suppose,' he said slowly, 'suppose Pizzoni didn't return the letters. What if the Ruffini family, installed in the farmhouse, saw your grandmother as the likely inheritor of anything Pizzoni had to leave? All they had to do was intercept the letters and send them back, giving him the idea that his daughter wanted nothing more to do with him?'

Nell considered this theory and then rejected it. 'I don't think so,' she said firmly. 'Italians are family people above all. Knowing how anguished her brother would have been by the loss of his son, Signora Ruffini would never have destroyed a link with his remaining child.'

Perhaps out of consideration for Giles, Middleton refrained from pointing out that there was no telling how people with Italian blood in their veins would react in normal situations, much less abnormal ones. So it was left to Jacqueline to seize on what Nell's confession really meant. Eyes sparkling and cheeks flushed, she announced that Sergio Ruffini was damned whatever happened.

'Either the Count finds the piece of paper we need — no certainty about that, I'm afraid — or Ruffini, who has got his bit of paper, is confronted by Pizzoni's direct descendant and the obvious inheritor of whatever property he owned.'

There followed, to Nell's ears, a deadly silence. Entranced with his daughter's reasoning, Frank Middleton didn't say anything at all; he merely smiled at so commendable a chip off the old Yorkshire block. Giles stared at his wife, and once again she felt deeply sorry for him; but not even for him could she let Jacqueline go unanswered.

'If I'm right in thinking you expect me to challenge Sergio Ruffini's ownership of the farm, I must make it clear that I shall do no such thing,' she said with absolute certainty. 'The matter is between him and Count Guidi; it has nothing to do with me.'

Jacqueline smiled as if it was the answer she'd been waiting for, then she looked at Giles. 'Poor you,' she murmured, 'what a bind to put you in — having to choose between us and your wife!'

He shook his head, like a horse tormented by summer flies. 'You and Frank both know, I hope, that I'm here to help you in any way I can; but Nell has to act as she sees fit — I can't change that.'

'Of course not,' Jacqueline agreed gently. 'She's free to choose not to help us, and we know she doesn't hold with our beautiful hotel. We'll manage without her.'

The girl was as agile as a cat, and just as ruthless, Nell realized, and Giles, blinded by infatuation for her and reverence for her father, would see nothing wrong with the company he was keeping. Sickened by that thought, she could find nothing more to say. She cast a despairing glance at him, got no response, and quietly left the room. Back in her bedroom, she discovered that her hands were trembling. Should she start to pack or wait to be asked to leave? By habit now, she went to stand at the window and let the peaceful beauty of the view calm her turmoil. No, she wouldn't go unless she had to; some instinct insisted that she was involved and had something still to do so that the bitterness and grief of the past could finally be laid to rest.

★　　★　　★

Another more peaceful conversation had also taken place after the Florentine lawyer's visit ended. On the way back through the garden to his own part of the house, wondering about the document he was supposed to find, Vittorio Guidi came across the woman he called Donna Joanna. Secateurs in hand, she was dead-heading a rose that had flung itself across the path into a self-sown white lilac that was now more tree than shrub. He gave his customary little bow and smiled at her.

'You can't bear the muddle,' he suggested, 'like Signora Nell!'

To his surprise, she shook her head and answered firmly. 'I love the muddle; it's how a garden ought to be – well almost! – not like the one we have at home, with everything planted by rule, so many of this and that to each square yard.' She pointed to the lovely copper-pink Albertine above her head. 'I'm only taking off the dead blooms so that many more buds will come.'

He noticed that she handled even the spent flowers gently, as if they were still precious; she was a gentle woman altogether, he realized, married to a man who perhaps didn't know the meaning of the word.

'You're without your friend today,' he said next. 'It's usually Signora Fanshawe that I find in the garden.'

'Nell's busy writing,' Joan explained. 'Books for children, which she illustrates herself. I think she's writing about this place; it's a magic garden, she says. I think she's right.' Joan's face, shadowed by the old straw hat she'd borrowed from Lucia, looked wistful, and he imagined her thinking of that other garden she didn't like back in Huddersfield. The word tolled in his mind, recalling him to what he was supposed to be doing.

'I must go indoors and search for a paper your husband needs,' he said regretfully, 'not hinder you from tidying up this jungle! I'm afraid Sir Frank is not pleased with a discussion we had this morning. A – what is the English word? – a hitch, I think, has occurred in his negotiations.'

Again she surprised him by shaking her head. 'He likes obstacles! At the moment, he's rather bored with the long rest he's been ordered to take; a difficulty or two is exactly what he needs!' She said it so earnestly that he burst out laughing, and then had to explain why.

'Do you wonder that we find the English so hard to understand?'

More seriously, he added, 'It doesn't affect our liking – Italians and English have always been friends, which is why we hated being on the wrong side in the last war – but our liking for each other is based on almost total misunderstanding on both sides. It's touching, I think, but also very funny!'

She found herself wanting him to go on talking, explaining things, sharing what went on in his mind, so that she might feel less ignorant about the strange, lovely place she'd come to. But, as if he suddenly remembered that he was a man who preferred a solitary life, he excused himself from dining with them that evening and said that he must get on with what he was meant to be doing indoors.

Alone again, she went back to the roses, feeling the double sadness of his loneliness and her own more acutely after that brief taste of companionship. But under the sadness ran a little seam of delight. For the first time in her life, she'd felt completely at ease with a man, and had sensed in him the same surprised pleasure. Life was sometimes unexpectedly sweet.

The midday meal on the terrace was consumed, and Beppe had brought coffee to the table when Frank Middleton fired a sudden question at Nell.

'These unknown relatives of yours – Ruffini and his grandson – are you going to get in touch with them, tell them who you are?'

Honesty forbade her to say that it was no concern of his; in the situation they were in, he had a right to know. If she were inclined to encourage the Ruffinis to obstruct what he wanted to do, he had a right to know that as well. 'I haven't made up my mind yet,' she said at last. 'If I decide to contact them, it will only be as Francesca's granddaughter; your affairs won't be mentioned. Does that sound fair?'

She saw Jacqueline about to protest and then Frank Middleton's small gesture to his daughter. 'It sounds completely fair,' he admitted, and for the first time Nell remembered what his wife had said about him: he was a fighter but he fought fairly. No doubt he'd got where he was by knowing when to trust the people he was dealing with.

When lunch was over, Giles cornered her alone for a moment. 'I'm sorry, Nell . . . sorry about this morning's interview . . . sorry about everything, in fact. Are you sure you wouldn't rather go home?'

'Until I'm made to feel unwelcome by Joan Middleton, I shall stay,' she answered. 'What Jacqueline thinks about my being here doesn't worry me very much.'

Rather to her surprise, a faint grin altered his face, making him familiar again. 'I'll say this for you, Mrs Fanshawe: anyone who tangles with you is in for a shock. Delicate as lace but tempered as steel; it's a formidable combination!'

'Good,' she agreed calmly. Then her own expression relaxed. 'I've had enough of the *famiglia* Middleton for a little while; I'm going to walk into Poggione to visit Signor Pavese. You could come too, but he only speaks Italian, and you look as if a snooze would be a good thing.'

'A swim first, then a snooze,' he amended, and she set off on her walk, trying not to think of a swim that he would almost certainly share with Jacqueline.

# Eight

She was in the middle of Poggione, almost before she was aware
of having walked the best part of a mile without noticing anything
that she passed along the way. Her mind was full of the discovery
of who was living at the farm down in the valley. Sergio Ruffini
must be much the same age as Francesca would have been now,
and his grandson, therefore, was of the same generation as Nell.
Had she learned of their existence in some other way than through
the morning's conversations, she wouldn't have hesitated to go
to the farm and claim them as relatives. But, as things were, it
was hard to see how it could be done without disclosing how
she came to be there. At least until Giles's professional dealings
with them were over, she would have to go on not knowing
them; and if the negotiations did become a war between the
Ruffinis and Middleton, she might never know them at all.

That much settled in her mind, she walked into Poggione's
wine store and chose a bottle of Chianti Classico that old Luciano
and his son might enjoy. Then, with this beautifully wrapped
up, she crossed the square and knocked at the door of the *presbiterio*. The woman who opened it, dressed in black and with
grey hair dragged back into a skimpy knot, was the archetypal
housekeeper, selected to raise no carnal longings in the priest
she looked after. But severity melted into a pleasant smile as
she explained that Signor Luciano was still unwell and his son
out visiting a parishioner. Nell left her gift and her good wishes
and said goodbye, then made for a shady seat at one of the
café's pavement tables – just the place to enjoy a cool drink
and watch the local world go by, awake again now after the
obligatory siesta.

Setting out afterwards to explore Poggione, she found that her
first impression of a lively, friendly town didn't need altering.
Butcher, baker, greengrocer, chemist – they were all there, along
with the experts who mended shoes, repaired watches, and even
built whatever items of furniture might be required. Poggione

was self-sufficient still, and all the better for that in Nell's considered opinion.

A tree-lined space at the end of a side street offered another resting place before she set off to walk back to the villa. But she was hardly there before it was invaded by a gang of teenagers bringing a ball to throw about between them; only a ball didn't mew piteously and have a tail. Nell leapt up and flung herself into the middle of them, intent on stopping the little cat from being kicked as it fell to the ground. In the stress of the moment, she shouted at its tormentors in English, and this at least directed attention away from the bedraggled heap that Nell had picked up.

'*Ha . . . Inglese . . . che stupida!*' the ringleader cried to the others who crowded round her, laughing and jeering; this was a better game of intimidation, it seemed. She was angry but beginning to feel frightened as well when something unexpected happened. A man she recognized came running towards them, hurling abuse in French. Not only that, but, with his newspaper rolled into an offensive weapon, he was already smiting the youth nearest to him.

With the leader under attack, there was a moment of indecision, and then some herd instinct made them all turn and run. The hubbub was suddenly over and Nell, with the cat still in her arms, was staring at a ruffled, white-faced Bertrand de la Tour.

'I can't imagine how you come to be here,' she said breathlessly, 'but you're more than welcome!'

'There's blood on your cheek, and your shirt is torn – those louts have hurt you.' He sounded so shaken and angry that she managed to smile at him.

'No, they didn't touch me – my small friend here was too terrified to tell rescuer from foe.'

He stared at her in silence, trying to get emotions under control again, and so she spoke again. 'I can't leave it here – it will starve to death even if those hooligans don't come back.'

'My hired car is parked at the end of the street – shall we go?' he suggested abruptly.

She nodded, supposing that he was embarrassed at having been seen outside his normal role of elegant, high-class professional. But seated in the car, with the little animal on her lap, she turned to look at him. 'Thank you for coming to our rescue. I couldn't understand what you were shouting, and probably nor could they, but it certainly did the trick!'

She couldn't read the expression on his face and wasn't prepared for what came next.

'It should have given me away,' he said quietly. 'Suddenly I was a child again – Jean Bottin, growing up in a Paris back-street slum far removed from what I live in now. My father had absconded and my mother worked like a slave to give me the best start she could. I was clever enough, thank God, to win scholarships, and determined to beat whatever opposition came my way. But it was my mother's idea that I should change my name – Bottin wouldn't do for the architect I knew I was going to be.'

He stopped suddenly, and Nell herself went on. 'I can finish the story. You became very, very successful and were able to take care of your mother in return.'

'Yes,' he agreed, 'until she died last year.' He turned to look at Nell. 'It's not a story I often tell.'

'Why should you?' she agreed calmly. 'But Sylvie knows, of course, I assume.'

'Yes, although I didn't tell her before we married – I should have done. When I did feel confident enough, it was too late; she's never forgiven me for the deception. Now we pose as man and wife, and work together as business partners.'

It explained a lot, Nell thought; it even made Sylvie seem human and understandable. Since that couldn't be said, though, she thought of something else. 'I should have liked to know your mother. Did she think up your new name or did you?'

A grin changed his face to one she suddenly liked. 'She chose Bertrand; de la Tour was my idea – we had a good laugh about it, I remember!'

Nell smiled back, picturing mother and son together. 'How *did* you come to be in Poggione this afternoon? You and Sylvie weren't at lunch.'

'I delivered her to stay with some grand friends for the night – people I don't like, so I pleaded work to do at the villa. On the way back I was looking for a watch repairer Beppe told me about – the strap on my watch had broken. Now, before that scruffy creature in your lap dies on us, we'd better be on our way.'

Nell touched one of its torn ears very gently. 'I won't let it die – some food and loving care and you won't recognize it in a day or two.'

She debated as they drove whether or not to mention the lawyer's visit that morning, then decided to leave Middleton and Giles to tell him about the obstacle that Sergio Ruffini was putting in their way. They went on in silence, but any hope of a quiet arrival was doomed by the sight of Lucia in the courtyard talking to a young man who had to be her and Beppe's son, Gianni. Exclamations of concern and horror rang out, bringing Carlotta running as well. The patient was handed over while Nell explained what was needed – warm milk first, followed by some food; then she was free to go indoors and escape to her room.

Someone, Bertrand she supposed, must have gone in search of Giles because he walked in a few minutes later, looking angry.

'I'm perfectly all right,' she said at once, correctly reading anger for concern. 'The only sad thing was that I'd been thinking how perfect Poggione was, and then suddenly it was like everywhere else – a mixture of good and bad.'

That sounded so like her that his frowning expression changed to one of exasperated tenderness. 'Dear Nell, it *was* a daft thing to do; you could have got seriously hurt – one stray cat that was probably going to starve to death anyway wasn't worth that.'

She thought of asking what, in his view, did merit taking a risk for, but it had been an emotional enough day already, and she felt too tired to argue. She simply smiled and said that she would lie down until it was time for dinner. As an afterthought, she added that Bertrand didn't know about their tangled relations with the Ruffini family. Giles nodded, then leaned down to kiss her scratched cheek.

'Battle honour,' he said gently. 'Now, love, go to sleep.'

Alone again, she took off her torn shirt and dirtied skirt, wrapped herself in a thin dressing gown, and lay down thankfully on the bed. Her last thought before falling asleep was that she wouldn't despair yet of keeping their marriage intact. Moments of tenderness like that one just now insisted that she still mattered to him enough for his present infatuation with Jacqueline to be a passing infection they could live through. It was a comforting idea to go to sleep with.

A note addressed to Giles in the Count's 'fine Italianate hand' was waiting on the hall table the following morning. It enclosed the only paper he had found relating to Luigi Pizzoni, dated 19 September 1944. Signed by Federico Guidi, it gave his tenant the right to regard the farm as his own for as long as he should live. Thereafter it would be part of the Guidi estate again. Giles muttered 'thank God', and went in to breakfast feeling that a weight had been lifted from his shoulders. Nothing could be clearer as to what the old Count's intentions had been, and no attempt to refute them could possibly succeed.

When Frank Middleton appeared, looking as if he hadn't slept well and needed the rest he was supposed to be having, Giles gave him the good news and said that he and Jacqueline would take the Count's document to Florence that morning. Then, together, they and the Count's lawyer would call on Sergio Ruffini.

It left the rest of them to fill in the day as they wished – Frank Middleton and Bertrand to discuss the hotel and the plans that the architect had begun to draw; Nell to check on the invalid in the kitchen – already showing signs of recovery – and then give Joan her Italian lesson. Afterwards, over coffee on the terrace as usual, they agreed that villa life had much to recommend it, particularly when Sylvie de la Tour happened to be elsewhere.

'It's an unkind thing to say,' Joan admitted, 'but didn't it seem to you that even Bertrand was more pleasant this morning, more content to be here?'

Knowing what she now knew, but had no permission to share, Nell could only agree that Joan was right but not account for it. 'At least, I suppose I can,' she said after a moment's thought. 'It seems clear now that the hotel will go ahead and Bertrand can really get down to work. I expect that's making him happy.'

Her companion nodded, but stared at her across the table. 'Since yesterday you've spoken about him in a different tone of voice; it isn't surprising after what happened in Poggione that you feel grateful, but it's more than that. I think you really like him now.'

'And so would you if you'd seen him clouting those beastly

teenagers,' Nell answered with a smile. 'But appearances are deceptive where Bertrand is concerned. I know him better now and like him very much.'

Joan hesitated for a moment and then risked her next question. 'If Sergio Ruffini is going to be made to leave, will that spoil things for you, Nell?'

'I don't see that it can do anything else,' was the honest answer she received, but when she looked distressed, Nell smiled at her. 'Don't let it upset you. Sergio and his family don't know I exist. In practical terms, as Jacqueline pointed out, they might prefer me not to exist; so it won't be a tragedy if I go back to England without getting to meet Francesca's relatives. But we'll know a bit more when Giles gets back.'

Joan nodded, then ventured on another worry. 'I warned you once before about Jacqueline, Nell. We'd both have to be blind not to see that she's . . . she's very taken with Giles. Who would not be? – he's an attractive man. But Frank is throwing them together because he knows she's got a lot to learn, and he wants her to know it before he has to give up himself. He's using Giles to teach her, not concerned, I'm afraid, that it might seem very unfair to you.'

Nell considered this honest statement for a moment before replying. 'What is unfair to me is that Jacqueline is nearly ten years younger, and is beautiful in a way that I have never been! But we can't do anything about that. My only hope is to *not* get shrill and whiney, and put my faith in Giles; I'm trying to look upon it as character building!' Her wry smile said more than her words did, and Joan knew that it was time to let the matter rest.

'I've got the Count's permission to snip and trim,' she said instead, 'so I shall borrow Beppe's secateurs again. I haven't had so much fun in a garden for years.'

'While I,' Nell answered, 'shall return to my pen and writing pad – so, *arrivederci*, Donna Joanna, as Vittorio calls you!' It was brave talk, but although she went to her little embowered table, she wrote no more than a paragraph before laying down her pen. There was too much more to think about than Seb's next adventure in his magic garden, and she was still idly sitting there when Carlotta came to find her and say that lunch was ready on the terrace.

# Nine

With Bertrand absent, collecting Sylvie from her grand friends, and Giles and Jacqueline closeted with the Count's lawyer, only Nell was there to join the Middletons at lunch – Lucia's delicious offering of cold fennel soup, stuffed peppers, and local cherries steeped in wine.

To help the conversation along, Nell reignited an earlier argument by asking Frank Middleton if he still thought Italian food lacking in finesse. But anticipating that Giles was in the process of worsting Sergio Ruffini, the great man was in jovial mood, ready to admit at least that what they were eating made a welcome change from pasta every day.

'Not that I don't like what she does with it,' he went so far as to say, 'but I'd rather see it in front of me now and then, not all the time.'

'You'd rather see roast beef and Yorkshire pudding in front of you,' Joan Middleton pointed out with a faint smile.

'Not here, not in this heat,' he contradicted her, but for once when he spoke to his wife he didn't sound irritable; and he even nodded when she reminded him more firmly than usual of the doctor's instruction that he must rest in the afternoon.

Nell listened with interest, aware that as Joan advanced a little in confidence, so her husband yielded a little ground. Her new-found assurance had something to do with the fact that she was beginning to feel and look well; but more important, in Nell's opinion, was her growing friendship with Vittorio Guidi. And since there was little that went on around him that Frank Middleton missed, Nell was pleasantly certain that he was taking notice of the Count's charming courtesy towards his wife.

She was thinking about this when a sudden question was fired at her across the table.

'If I'm right in thinking Giles isn't going to mention your connection with the family when he goes to the farm, why does it matter?'

'He won't mention it, and it probably doesn't matter,' Nell answered slowly. 'What does matter is Sergio Ruffini's connection with my great-grandfather.'

'Meaning what exactly?' Middleton asked.

'Meaning that Luigi Pizzoni hated Count Federico – blamed him for the sacrifice of his son's life. Family relationships are everything here, and if Sergio can hold up a sale that will benefit Federico's grandson, he will think it's what family honour requires him to do.'

Frank Middleton considered this for a moment. 'So in your opinion we're not yet home and dry?'

'It probably depends on how successful the farm is,' Nell answered. 'If Sergio is struggling to make a living, he might just agree to be bought out, provided you deal with him fairly; if not, not.'

Middleton smiled, about to pounce on the flaw in her reasoning. 'I'd agree with you but for a small, important item: I've got the document that proves who the farm belongs to – the Count, not Ruffini.'

It was Nell's turn to pause before she spoke again. 'Whatever your paper says, doesn't it count for something that Sergio has devoted his life to the farm, believing that it belongs to him?'

'Now you're being sentimental,' came the answer. 'Belief is one thing; legality is something else altogether. But, in spite of holding the winning card, I *shall* be generous, and Ruffini can go and farm elsewhere if he wants to.'

Nell held up her hands in a little gesture of defeat. 'We aren't going to agree, so I shall save my breath to cool my porridge – I'm sorry, I don't know a Yorkshire way of saying that, but you're well aware anyway that I think this lovely countryside should be left to Tuscan people.' Then she stood up and smiled at Joan. 'I'm off for a swim before Sylvie gets back in time to tell me that my way of doing the crawl is all wrong!'

Middleton waited for her to walk away before he spoke again. 'She's daft, but she's a mettlesome piece,' he commented.

'She's the kindest, dearest person I've ever met,' his wife said bravely. 'I can't allow you to criticize her to me.'

'I was paying her a compliment,' he replied before he, too, walked away.

★   ★   ★

Now into the month of June, the evening was warm enough for Beppe to set out pre-dinner drinks on the terrace. It was a time of day that Nell loved, and she changed early and went outside happy to find herself alone there. The sun had dipped below the distant line of hills, but in its afterglow she could watch the changing colours of the sky – orange, pink, lilac, and finally grape-purple as the first stars came out.

She was still alone when Giles walked out and sat down beside her. He looked tired, and she saw the effort that was needed for him to smile at her. She wanted to smooth the tension lines about his mouth, wanted to say, 'Dear Giles, let's forget this Tuscan visit and go home,' but what they were involved in was too compli-cated for that.

'Talk if you want to,' she said instead. 'If not, just relax and wait for the nightingales to sing.'

He touched her hand briefly, but didn't answer at once. 'We've been back a little while,' he explained at last, 'but I had to talk to Frank first. He agreed that the rest of you should know how far our negotiations have got – Bertrand and Sylvie are involved, obviously; you have a close connection, and so, of course, does Vittorio Guidi. I am to bring you all up to date when dinner is over.'

'And I am meant to ask no questions in the meanwhile. I can recognize a gentle hint when I hear one!'

A faint smile acknowledged this before he went on. 'Well, there's something I do need to talk about now. Frank wants me to leave Marchants and join him – become his troubleshooter-in-chief. It would mean a seat on the board – the whole works, in fact.' He saw the dismay in her face and hurried on. 'A year ago I was simply one of the firm's team of corporate lawyers – it's a tremendous compliment. Can you put aside your feelings about him enough to understand that?'

Nell saw that her hands were shaking and hid them in the pockets of her skirt. 'What I understand is that he's trying to buy you, body and soul. Have you accepted his offer?'

'How could I, without talking to you?' He lifted his hand to delay what he guessed she was about to say. 'Please think about it, Nell. Such an opportunity won't come my way again, and I'd be judged insane to turn it down.'

At this crucial moment they were interrupted by the arrival of Bertrand and his wife, and Nell made a huge effort to pull herself together sufficiently to hope that Sylvie had enjoyed the visit to her friends.

The Frenchwoman's face glowed with remembered pleasure. 'Such food, such conversation! It was wonderful to be among true intellectuals again.'

In the silence that followed this statement, Nell tried to stifle a giggle, but Giles's horrified glance at her only made matters worse; she had to laugh or burst before she could explain that she was not on the verge of becoming hysterical. It was Bertrand – her saviour for the second time – who came to her rescue. He stepped in front of her while she mopped her eyes, but spoke to his affronted wife.

'*Chérie*, Nell thought you were joking. You should know by now that the English don't take intellectuals seriously. We think they're cultural heathens; they think we're pretentious eggheads – so much for the Entente-not-very-Cordiale!'

Precariously balanced on the edge of collapsing again, Nell looked gratefully at him and then turned to Sylvie. 'Forgive me, please. It's quite true what Bertrand said – we have a deplorable habit of laughing at things we shouldn't laugh at.' And even as she spoke the words, she felt assailed by sadness instead. Time was when Giles would have found Sylvie de la Tour as much of an entertainment as she did; but no longer. He'd been hooked and reeled in to this high-octane, unreal world he now inhabited. She had no doubt that he would accept Frank Middleton's offer.

The next interruption to the conversation was more welcome. The Count arrived, followed by all three Middletons, Jacqueline practically incandescent in lime-green and happily aware of its effect against her tanned skin and dark hair. Ever since Sylvie's lecture on black for evening wear, she'd appeared in one vibrant colour after another – an act of rebellion that even Nell approved of.

They went indoors to dinner. After the food and then coffee had been served, Frank Middleton addressed the meeting.

'It's time to tell you how things stand. I already own two thirds of the land we need for the hotel and its surrounding grounds. This morning, armed with the Count's document relating to the status of the remaining third, Giles expected to return with Sergio

Ruffini's farm in his pocket as well. I'll let him tell you what happened.'

Nell watched her husband stand up, a tall, elegant man compared with the burly figure beside him; a clever, ambitious man whose training told him that legality was entirely on the side of his client, and so, in the cut and thrust of high commerce, sentiment would have to bow its head and die.

'Count Vittorio found for us his grandfather's written state-ment of intent – the farm worked by a tenant, Luigi Pizzoni, would be during his lifetime *as if* he owned it – no rent, no share of produce required by the *padrone*. But at his death it would return to the Guidi estate. With no child to succeed him, Pizzoni invited his sister and brother-in-law to help him work the farm, but, while still alive, he willed the farm to his relative-by-marriage, Sergio Ruffini, who now regards it as his. It is a clear case of malfeasance, but only a judge can weigh both sides of the argu-ment. I have no doubt that he will pronounce in favour of the Count. Meanwhile, we cannot evict Ruffini, and the legal system here grinds just about as slowly as the wheels of God.'

In the silence that followed, Nell glanced round the room. Bertrand and Sylvie seemed to be asking a question of each other, and the Count looked withdrawn into some speculation of his own. It was Frank Middleton who spoke first.

'Ruffini is laughing at us, of course; reckons a wily Italian can outsmart an Englishman any day. I expect to prove him wrong.'

Then Vittorio Guidi's quiet voice was heard. 'Ruffini's target, Sir Frank, is me, I'm afraid. Luigi Pizzoni's hatred of my family has been passed on to him, and he imagines that the sale of the farm would make me a rich man. Added to that, there is the grandson who apparently wishes to continue farming, something I was not aware of when you first approached me.'

Another pause occurred, broken this time by Jacqueline. 'The judge will need to be told that Pizzoni's only remaining blood relative is *here*.' She smiled sweetly at Nell. 'This legal heir *is* on our side, I hope?'

It was Giles who now felt obliged to intervene, but he turned to look at Middleton, not at Jacqueline. 'Nell did make it clear that she's not prepared to try to oust Ruffini – she believes right is on his side even if the law is on ours.'

With every pair of eyes in the room focused on her, Nell struggled to keep her voice steady. 'I refuse to make any claim on the farm, now or in the future. All I *will* do is call on Sergio Ruffini, explain who I am, and assure him that payment for the farm would go to *him*. The Count would be the loser, and, of course, I should need his permission.'

Jacqueline jumped to her feet, eyes blazing. 'No, that won't do,' she almost shouted. 'Pizzoni was a cheat and so is his brother-in-law; we can't let them win.'

Giles smiled at her. 'You're right, of course, partner, but now we have to let Count Guidi decide.'

Vittorio ignored them both and spoke to Nell. 'My permission is given,' he said gravely. 'I want neither Ruffini's farm nor Sir Frank's payment for it.' And his tone of voice suggested that there the discussion would end.

Jacqueline's radiant smile embraced both Giles and her father. 'Well, there you are, then; it's all fixed.'

Frank Middleton turned to Bertrand. 'Certainly fixed enough for you and Sylvie to carry on – there's a mountain of work ahead of you.' Then he remembered that Nell had some part to play in what happened next. 'It's a mercy you can tackle Ruffini in his own language – try to make him understand that what I'm doing is in the interests of the people in this run-down bit of Tuscany.'

'I shall do my best,' she said, without committing herself as to what Tuscany really needed, and after that it was a relief when the meeting broke up and she could say goodnight and escape upstairs.

When Giles appeared some time later, she was already in bed, trying to enjoy a current novel she had no interest in. He looked relaxed for once, presumably sharing Jacqueline's view that, between them, the problem of Sergio Ruffini could now be fixed.

She prayed that he wouldn't talk about it, wouldn't – much worse still – feel that he must make love to her as a reward for reasonably good behaviour. To have him touch her and pretend that it was Jacqueline beneath his hands would be more than she could bear. In order to avoid that, she would even return to the conversation that had been interrupted.

'Are you going to leave Marchants?' she suddenly asked. 'The pricking in my thumbs tells me that you are.'

The coolness in her voice warned him that he would not be welcome in her bed, but innate honesty made clear to him the reason why. Instead of answering her question, he asked one of his own. 'I suppose you know that Bertrand is falling in love with you? I hope it isn't as obvious to Sylvie as it is to me.'

'We're simply trying to promote better Anglo-French under-standing,' Nell said solemnly. 'She surely can't object to that?' Then her voice changed. 'You didn't answer my question.'

'I don't know the answer yet,' he answered.

'I expect you soon will,' came the soothing reply. She gave a little yawn and laid down her book. 'Really, this is a most tedious novel – do you suppose publishers simply lie when they splatter jackets with "number one best-seller" slogans?' She yawned again, and Giles crossed the room to switch off her bedside light.

'I've no idea what publishers do,' he replied briefly, 'but don't let *my* uncertainties keep you awake.'

She smiled sleepily at him and turned her head into one of Lucia's soft pillows; there would be time enough to lie awake and weep when the room was in darkness and he was sound asleep.

# Ten

It had become a habit now – a cup of coffee shared with Lucia and Beppe in the kitchen, and then a quiet hour outside before anyone else was likely to be about. Nell roamed the different terraced levels, thinking that this solitary morning ritual would be her happiest memory of a summer like no other. But halted in front of a new discovery, the delicate statue of a little fawn, one leg raised as if he was about to run away, she found once again that Vittorio Guidi was also an early riser.

To avoid returning to the previous evening's conversation, she pointed to the small stone figure in front of her.

'I was about to sketch him,' she confessed. 'I write and illustrate books for children, and I'm concocting a story about this magical garden, in which all these little stone animals come to life. I hope you don't mind.' She didn't add that in her story they would become the playmates of a lonely boy, as the man beside her had been.

The Count didn't seem to mind at all. '*Il giardino segreto* was an Italian invention,' he said with his charming smile. 'Your story should be translated for our children to read.' He glanced around as if surprised by the garden's wild beauty, and Nell risked the question that was in her mind.

'Do you hate us being here? I think you might – you're a very private man.'

He looked at her now with sadness, considering what she'd said. 'You could more truthfully have called me a very selfish man. Since my father died, I've shut not only myself but all this away from other people. You and Donna Joanna have made me look at what is here, what needs to be done.' Then, when Nell didn't answer, he asked a question of his own.

'You're troubled, I think? Torn between finding yourself very much at home here and hating what you're now caught up in. If any of your concern is for me, I promise you that it needn't be.'

Nell's face relaxed into a smile. '"And they shall be accounted poet-*kings*,"' she quoted, '"who only tell the most heart-easing things"! John Keats said that, but I'm sure you knew it already.'

He indicated a nearby bench and led her to it. When they were sitting down, he spoke again. 'I don't think you like what has been forced on you – the visit to Sergio Ruffini.'

She nodded and suddenly began to tell him Francesca's story. 'My great-grandfather was a brave man,' she finally finished up, 'but life made him vindictive – not only to your family but to his daughter as well.' She looked at her companion. 'The war was more than half a century ago, but the tragic stain of it still seeps into what happens now. I suppose I dread going to the farm because I can't decide whether I'm raking up the pain of the past or laying it to rest.' She managed to smile at the Count. 'If Sergio Ruffini won't listen to me and I have to report failure, Jacqueline for one will say that it's because I'm on the wrong side! She knows what I feel about her father's project.'

Vittorio shook his head. 'Middleton himself is a better judge of character. I think he knows that you wouldn't be disloyal to your husband, whatever you felt about the hotel.' His shy smile peeped out again. 'Far from hating your being here, I have to admit that life has suddenly become much more interesting! I shouldn't say that when there are –' he hesitated over the word to use '– problems that must be resolved, but I assure you, *cara* Nell, that I regard this as an adventure that has brought me un-expected friends.'

She was touched by what he said, aware that the agreeable Italian habit of making statements simply to give pleasure wasn't something that would occur to him; what he said was what he meant.

'Time to go indoors,' she decided reluctantly. 'Carlotta will have breakfast ready, and I've thought up a deep philosophical question to ask Sylvie – she feels, poor love, that her present companions aren't nearly intellectual enough!'

Vittorio shook his head in wonderment. 'You are a strange race, you English – she insults you and you laugh or feel sorry for her!'

'There's no making us out at all,' Nell agreed, almost by way of apology; then she stood up, holding out her hand to say goodbye.

He watched with pleasure as she walked away, a long-legged

girl who moved with the free grace of a dancer, then he sat down again, to think about the wartime story she had told him, and the likely outcome of her visit to the farm. It hinged, probably, on Marco Ruffini. If Sergio was simply using him to make Middleton offer more money, he would agree in the end. But if his grandson was serious about keeping the farm going, then Nell's visit would simply stir up old quarrels that were better left alone. Feeling anxious about her himself, he would have been surprised to know that Giles was also regretting the corner she'd been driven into by the Middletons.

At least with Jacqueline absent from the breakfast table, Giles could smile a welcome at his wife. 'Night-owl to lark – are you receiving me? Did you find the worm that the early bird is supposed to catch?'

'I found Count Vittorio,' she answered cheerfully. 'He likes the garden in the dawning as much as I do. He's a very nice man, and I now feel free to consider him a friend.'

Giles waited for Carlotta to bring fresh coffee and rolls to the table, then spoke more seriously. 'Nell, I don't like you going to see Ruffini alone – in fact, I'd rather you didn't have to go at all; at least I think I ought to be with you.'

She smiled at him but shook her head. 'Wouldn't that defeat the object? I'm going as distant relative, not as part of the Middleton camp.' But the concern in her husband's face made her go on. 'The worst that can happen is a door shut in my face, but I don't even expect that. At least by Jacqueline's reasoning, I've more right to be there than he has.' She hesitated for a moment. 'Tell me honestly, please: had my great-grandfather any legal permission to leave things as he did?'

'My dear, I can't answer that,' Giles admitted. 'Count Federico's intention was clear enough, but God alone knows how an Italian judge would interpret the law. Our best hope is that Sergio's target is Vittorio Guidi; if the Count is not to benefit from the sale, he may very well do a deal with us.'

Nell nodded and poured herself more coffee. 'I'll accept a lift to the farm but I'd like to walk back. I don't think you should be seen loitering!' Then she smiled at what she'd said. 'All this intrigue – it's becoming silly; we're not living in fourteenth-century Florence.'

'No, but we *are* dealing with wily Tuscans who, as Frank says, would like to get the better of what they see as simple-minded Anglo-Saxons!'

She didn't argue the point, now thinking about something else. 'If Sergio is the son of Luigi's younger sister, he's likely to be nearly as old as Francesca would be – say, approaching eighty. He can't, surely, be doing much of the farm work himself, so I can expect *him* to be at home when I call, even if Marco Ruffini isn't there.'

Giles stared at her for a moment, suddenly wishing they weren't at the villa at all, that the clock could be put back and they were still the young man and woman who'd fallen in love in a London car park over a supermarket trolley. Regret made his voice sharp when he spoke again.

'Have you thought what you're going to say to Ruffini – how you're even going to start?'

Nell answered calmly enough. 'I shall start with the truth. We were told nothing by Francesca; I saw the tablet in the church, and Luciano Pavese explained to me what it meant. The rest he'll know that I've learned from the Count's lawyer – I can't pretend that I'm not staying at the villa.' She hesitated before going on. 'Giles, about leaving Marchants—'

It was as far as she got before he held up his hand. 'Leave it for the moment, Nell. Frank isn't hurrying me for an answer, and we'll see what happens here first. If it doesn't work out, he may want to withdraw his offer anyway. Just go and meet your long-lost relations – I hope they make you welcome.'

Her smile thanked him, but all she said was, 'I'll see you in the courtyard in half an hour. I don't want to be here when the others appear – I think I might manage better without their advice!'

It was a short drive; within a few minutes of leaving the villa, Giles stopped the car at a track leading off the main road.

'You can see the farmhouse from here,' he said. 'You can't get lost – the track only leads to the farm and then stops.' He leaned over and kissed her cheek. 'If you insist on walking back, I'll be waiting for you at the villa.'

She got out, waved goodbye, and walked towards a house typical of its kind all over Tuscany – handsomely built of stone, it had the usual outside staircase leading to the upper floor where the family would once have lived while the livestock were housed beneath them. But here the ground floor had been converted into pleasant living quarters as well. An archway at one side led to the yard and the farm buildings. This was no rural slum – everywhere spoke of care and good management, and she lifted the heavy knocker on the door with the feeling that she was wasting her time and Sergio Ruffini's as well. Why would he be persuaded to leave what he so clearly cherished?

The door in front of her remained obstinately shut, and she gave up on the house and walked under the archway instead. The buildings around the yard spoke their purposes clearly enough – cantina, olive press, stables and barn. The sound of hammering led her to the last of these, and there, working at a bench was an elderly, thickset man that she guessed to be Ruffini himself. When the hammering ceased for a moment, she called out.

'*Buon giorno, Signore. Posso entrare?*'

He spun round to stare at the slender, unItalian-looking woman who smiled uncertainly at him from the doorway.

He put down his tool and came towards her, and, even in working clothes, he was far from being the peasant farmer she realized she'd been expecting. He was a handsome old man – something else Giles had omitted to mention – and his gaze was piercingly direct, questioning what she was doing there.

Struggling for once to find the Italian words she wanted, Nell explained that she was the granddaughter of Francesca Pizzoni, on a visit to Tuscany from England. She added that he no doubt knew that Francesca had married the English soldier her family had sheltered during the war, and gone to live with him in London.

'Yes, I knew that,' he agreed briefly. 'With Franco dead, it left her father alone here.'

Nell gestured at his bench. 'If you aren't too busy, may I talk to you for a few minutes?'

He hesitated for a moment, almost about to refuse, and then suddenly changed his mind. 'We'll talk indoors, not here.'

She followed him across the yard to a door at the rear of the farmhouse and then into a large kitchen which probably served as eating and sitting room as well. It was almost clinically neat and clean – evidence, Nell thought, of a woman about the house who was not Sergio Ruffini's wife. There was nothing to indicate that love went into its tending – no flowering geraniums on the windowsills, no stockpot simmering on the stove.

A chair at the long table was pulled out for her, and Nell sat down. Then, before saying anything, she took out of her pocket the photograph Luciano Pavese had sent her and laid it on the table.

'I went into the church in Poggione and saw the wall tablet,' she began. 'The priest's father explained to me what had happened. Until then I didn't even know that this was where my grandmother had lived, but when Signor Pavese told me about Franco, I finally understood why all her letters to her father had been returned. I only found them after she was dead.'

The man opposite her sat with his hands folded in front of him on the table, his face as nearly expressionless as an Italian's could be. 'If you didn't know about Poggione, why did you come here?' he asked. 'There's nowhere to stay here, nothing to see.'

The hurdle of the truth was in front of her now, and Nell could think of no way to avoid it. 'I'm staying at the villa,' she answered slowly. 'You've already met my husband, Giles Fanshawe. He came here with Count Guidi's lawyer.'

She waited for an explosion that didn't come; instead, Sergio Ruffini leaned back in his chair, considering what she'd just told him. At last he gave a little nod. 'So now I understand why you're here. Your clever husband is suggesting that, as Luigi Pizzoni's great-granddaughter, you should have inherited the farm.' When Nell didn't immediately answer, he stared at her with fierce, bright eyes. 'We are playing a game of chess, *non è vero*? It's your move now, Signora.'

She shook her head. 'We aren't playing a game at all. As I understand it, my great-grandfather gave the farm to you before he died. The question is whether he had any legal right to do so, or whether it should have reverted to the Guidi estate. That is something a judge would have to decide, if either I or Count Vittorio wanted the farm. I'm here simply to tell you that we don't. You are free to accept Sir Frank Middleton's offer or turn it down.'

There was another pause – Sergio plotting *his* next move, she supposed. Then he shook his head. 'I don't think so. There are title deeds which *il Signor Conte* still has. He would let me sell the farm, no doubt, and then demand the money.'

The explosion now came unexpectedly from Nell. She even startled him by banging the table. 'That's not fair and not true,' she said with all the force she could muster. 'Luigi Pizzoni blamed the Count's grandfather for his son's death, but it happened more than sixty years ago – isn't that too long to nurse hatred and distrust? Vittorio Guidi will *give* you the deeds' – a sudden glimmer of amusement lit her face – 'at least, he will if he can find them; he isn't a very organized landowner!'

Her rueful honesty brought a change in the atmosphere, and it was her turn to be surprised, because Sergio stood up and went to fetch glasses and a bottle from the refrigerator. Unaccustomed to drinking at mid-morning, she looked hesitant, but he pushed a filled glass towards her.

'Drink it – it's good; our own vintage.' He took a sip himself, and then returned to the matter in hand.

'I don't know your name, the name your mother gave you.'

'Eleanora,' Nell said, 'but it's too long for every day – people call me Nell.'

He raised his glass in a little gesture of apology. 'Very well then, Nell – I believe what you say because your eyes are honest, and I have no real reason not to trust the present Count. But there remains a problem for your husband and his English *padrone*: we – my grandson and I – have no intention of selling this farm. We have the intention of *staying* – of improving the quality of our wine and our olive oil year by year, as we have been doing ever since Luigi died.'

Given the chance, she would have kissed him and wished him well, but she had come to do her best for Giles. 'I understand what you say,' she answered earnestly, 'but isn't it possible that, with what Sir Frank would pay you, an even better farm could be bought – one that is easier to work perhaps?'

He looked at her almost pityingly. 'In Tuscany? No farm can be easy here, but we are used to that. We work it as we must and, preserved by God from disease and bad weather at the wrong times of year, we can do well enough.'

Nell sipped her wine, found it good and told him so. Then

she returned to what he'd just said. 'Not everyone agrees with you, I'm afraid. There *are* derelict farmhouses here and untended land – even your nearest neighbours have gone.'

Sergio nodded. 'They'd no one to help them carry on. I have Marco, and I thank God for him every day. You should meet him, but he's got strong ideas of his own – doesn't hold with the old order of things. Everyone's equal in his view; I expect your husband would call him a communist.'

Nell privately reckoned that even if Giles didn't, Frank Middleton certainly would, but, instead of saying so, she only pointed out that they were cousins of some distant sort who ought to know each other. 'We don't have to talk politics!' she ended up with a smile.

He was about to agree when the shadow of a man fell across the kitchen's open doorway, and then the man himself walked in. Taller than the average Italian, burnt brown by wind and sun, he could only be Marco Ruffini. He stared at the wine glasses on the table and then at Nell, but his stern expression didn't relax into a smile.

Sergio hurried to make the introduction. 'Marco, meet Luigi's great-granddaughter, Eleanora—' It was as far as he got before he was interrupted.

'The wife of Signor Fanshawe, I believe,' Marco said stiffly. 'I heard from Gianni that you were staying at Villa Guidi. Luigi Pizzoni would never have forgiven you for that.' He spoke, she thought, as much to his grandfather as to herself, reminding him not to fraternize with the enemy. Then, before she could think of something to say, he offered her a brief nod and walked back into the yard again.

It was Nell who broke the silence he left behind. '*Very* strong views of his own,' she suggested ruefully, 'and not about to listen to anyone else's! I'd better leave, I think; then he'll be able to come indoors again.' She saw the embarrassment in Sergio's face but shook her head. 'It doesn't matter – I've said what I came to say; now I'll leave you to talk to the lawyers. In spite of everything, I'm still glad I came to Tuscany and filled in the gaps in Francesca's story.'

She picked up her photograph and got to her feet. Sergio stood up too, clearly unhappy now.

'I'm sorry – you must forgive my grandson. He isn't normally rude, but the lawyers who came here were too confident for his liking. They made it plain they thought we shouldn't be here . . . that we were only waiting to be bought out. But Marco loves this place and he'll fight anyone who tries to take it away from us.'

Nell's smile reassured him. 'Thank goodness a young man of his age *does* feel like that – Tuscany needs a few more of them!' She hesitated for a moment before going on. 'I won't come again. Marco sees me as belonging with the people he dislikes, but there's nothing I can do about that.'

Sergio stared at her and slowly nodded his head. 'You look much more English than Italian, but you remind me of Francesca when you smile. I was two years younger than she was, but I remember her very well.'

'Signor Pavese said that, too,' Nell answered. 'No wonder she was missed so much.'

They walked together round to the front of the farmhouse, and, on a sudden impulse, she leaned over to kiss him goodbye. Then, without looking back, she walked away from what had been Francesca's home.

Sergio's hand touched his cheek for a moment as he watched her go, and he remembered something she'd said, or, more nearly, shouted at him. It should have been time to bury the tragedies of the past, but they still weren't dead, not by a long way. Because of them, he and Marco had refused Nell Fanshawe the welcome she deserved. They wouldn't get a second chance; she'd go back to London and never remember again that a small part of her properly belonged here.

# Eleven

She would have liked more time than the walk back to the villa allowed to think about the last half-hour. Could her visit have ended differently if she'd approached Sergio Ruffini in some other way? But Marco's hostility made the answer to that clear: if *she* hadn't done very well in getting on terms with her relatives, Giles and the Count's lawyer had done a good deal worse.

She tried not to dawdle, aware that they would be waiting for her, but when she reached the villa courtyard, she was confronted by Jacqueline, not Giles.

'They're very *engagés*,' she announced in her usual take-it-or-leave-it fashion. 'Tell me what happened and I'll pass it on.'

Nell called silently to heaven to help her remain outwardly calm. With that superhuman aid, she even managed to smile at this girl she'd come to dislike so profoundly.

'Thank you, but I think I'll do the passing-on myself.' The smile didn't reach her eyes, and Jacqueline – in whom the instinct to survive to fight another day was strong – merely shrugged and followed her into the house.

Giles got up as Nell entered the room – as did the Count's lawyer – and pulled out a chair for her. With the spark of anger still in her face, he assumed that her reception at the farm had been unpleasant.

'All right, Nell?' he asked quickly.

'I'm all right, but my visit achieved precisely nothing,' she answered.

Jacqueline began to say, 'Surprise, surprise—' but it was as far as she got before Nell interrupted her.

'I'd rather tell you what happened without any interruptions,' she said pointedly. After a glance at his daughter, Middleton nodded, and Nell went on with her story.

'Sergio Ruffini was suspicious of me at first but he gradually accepted what I was saying – that Count Guidi and I made no claim on the farm; he was free to sell it how and when he liked.

But on that point he was adamant: there would be no sale because he and his grandson were determined to go on running the farm – *that* farm, not one anywhere else. At that moment his grandson walked in, and, at the sight of me, almost immediately walked out again. Beppe's son had told him that I belonged here with the people who imagined that the offer of money would buy them whatever they asked for.' She stared across the room at Frank Middleton. 'I'm afraid that *no* amount of money will get you my great-grandfather's farm – it isn't for sale.'

It was tempting to add that she privately rejoiced in the fact, but Giles's disappointed face suggested that he already had enough to contend with; an aberrant wife as well would be altogether too much. She looked round the now-silent room, then walked out into the garden to pass the time of a very troubled day with her friends, the little laughing boy and his dolphin.

It was there that Giles found her, floating leaves in the clear water the dolphin now swam in.

'You were angry indoors,' he said. 'Now you look defeated. Is that how you feel?'

'I don't know *how* I feel,' she answered, 'apart from finding divided loyalties very uncomfortable things to have. I know Jacqueline distrusts me, but I truly didn't let it show that I wanted Sergio to hold out against bribery or brute force. Can't Frank Middleton build his blasted hotel somewhere else?'

'Not willingly, Nell. He's a man with a dream to realize. He reckons he's found the perfect spot, and he's already made a large investment in it. There's no doubt he would be generous – the Ruffinis could take their pick of empty farms in Tuscany.'

She held up her hands in despair. 'They don't *want* their pick – they just want to keep what they've toiled over and cherished for years. Can't *you* at least understand that, even if the Middletons can't?'

She read the expression in his face and gave him no chance to speak. 'If you're about to tell me that there's no place for senti-ment in today's world, I shall know for certain what I've feared for some time: you and I no longer inhabit yesterday's world, which I much prefer to this one.'

He answered after a moment, sounding stiff. 'We're talking now about ourselves, I take it, not about the hotel?' She nodded but let him go on. He did his best to seem patient and forbearing. 'Nell, we've had this argument before – my professional responsibilities versus your inclinations and personal dislike of Frank Middleton. I don't know how we reconcile them; do you?'

'We probably can't,' she answered, 'but it *isn't* what we're talking about. It's probably obvious to everyone else, and it certainly is to me, that your loyalty to him is confused with your feelings for his daughter. I promised myself I'd never say this, but I know in my very bones every time you look at her who it is that you want.'

She had no idea what his response would be, beyond the certainty that he wouldn't lie to her. At last he found something to say. 'I can't deny the . . . the chemistry, Nell; it just happens to be there. Could you try to look on it as . . . as a passing thing, not important enough to wreck us?'

'I might,' she answered slowly, 'if I could be sure it *was* a fever you'd recover from. But the only way to find that out is to do what you want to do – sleep with her. Then all three of us might know whether there's more to it than simple lust. For Joan Middleton's sake, I wouldn't ask you to move out of my bedroom; she's conditioned to believing that anything that goes wrong is somehow her fault.'

She knew that she was talking too much, but if she didn't talk, she'd have to weep. Then the leaves her fingers were destroying were swept out of her hands as Giles grabbed hold of them.

'Nell, you've got some of it wrong,' he insisted. 'Not my part in it; I'm to blame for that. But Jacqueline isn't the heartless tramp you think she is. Frank's illness threw us together, and we were caught unawares, but she wouldn't sleep with me even if I suggested it – she has her own code and sticks to it.'

'So what do you suggest instead?' Nell asked unevenly.

'That we get through this visit – my professional future depends on it – and sort ourselves out when we get home. I know it's a lot to ask. Can you possibly manage it?'

She pulled her hands free and nodded, unable to look at him. 'A marriage of convenience – isn't that what it's called? We might have done better on that Scottish holiday we were going to have. Perhaps there's something unavoidably fateful about Tuscany!'

'We may still do better when we leave,' he suggested hoarsely and then walked away from a conversation he could no longer bear.

She stayed where she was, listening in her mind to what Shakespeare had suggested in some dark, bitter moment of his life:

'Past reason hunted and, no sooner had,
Past reason hated.'

He'd known a great deal about human nature, the Man from Stratford, but he gave her little comfort now. She'd made Giles face the truth, but not the whole truth, because in his present state it seemed pointless to warn him of the future she foresaw. Abetted by her father, Jacqueline would play him on her line until his marriage was beyond saving. Then, with wealth and the inheritance of a business empire dangled in front of him, he would belong completely to the Middletons.

Facing that prospect, Nell was reminded of the moment – a lifetime ago it seemed now – when she'd decided to murder Eleanor Fanshawe and become herself again. What a useless little gesture it had turned out to be, or, at least, if the gesture had been right, how heartbreakingly futile subsequent events had made it.

The conversation at lunch was strained, despite Sylvie's well-meant attempt to enliven it by suggesting that the French President should become the permanent President of the European Union. Immersed as he was in thought, even Frank Middleton ignored the fly cast over him, apart from growling, '*That* pocket-Napoleon? I think not.'

No one seemed to linger over Lucia's delicious meal, and Nell soon found refuge in one of the garden's many hiding places. With pad and pencil idle in her lap, she was trying to think of nothing at all when a gentle touch on her wrist made her open her eyes. Bertrand stood there, not sure whether he was welcome.

'I'll go away if you'd rather I did,' he said. 'The others have been given permission by the boss to disport themselves in the pool, but I never learned to swim. Instead of admitting it, I pretended that it was a boring way to spend an afternoon – a pointless fib; Sylvie will have given me away by now.'

Nell made room on the seat beside her and turned to smile at him.

'What else have you to confess? Since you seem in a confessing mood! You think the Pompidou Centre in Paris is an eyesore, you loathe escargots, and refuse ever to man a single barricade! Anything else?'

It occurred to him then and there to confess to something that wasn't a fib – that in the space of less than a week he'd met and fallen in love with her. But there'd been sadness in her face when he arrived, and now was surely the time for another point-less fib instead.

'I'm longing for someone to look at my design for a hotel that I gather may now never be built, and tell me how beautiful it is.' He opened the folder he'd brought with him and handed her the first sketch. It was a detailed, exquisite drawing of a Tuscan *castello*, set against a backdrop of wooded hills and snow-tipped mountains.

'It's more than beautiful – it's perfect,' Nell said at once. 'And now I'm terribly torn, because I don't want the hotel built! This should be the glorious home of a large and happy Tuscan family. Sir Frank has enough land already, surely, to have it built and live in it himself. But, alas, he has only one daughter, and I very much doubt whether he would choose to make his home in Italy.' She studied the drawing again and then smiled at Bertrand. 'Is it true that most architects end up forsaking buildings for painting pictures?'

'Some do,' he admitted, 'but I just want to do what I do – create something that can be beautifully realized in glass and brick and stone but fulfil its purpose as well.'

'It's a good enough ambition,' she agreed gently. 'But what's going to happen – do you know?'

Bertrand gave a little shrug. 'The great man is plunged in thought, I gather. He thrives on opposition, positively enjoys a fight; but it's hard to see what that can do for him now unless the Count agrees to challenge Ruffini's ownership of the farm.'

'Vittorio Guidi won't do that,' Nell said certainly. 'If pushed to it, I think he'd agree with Marco Ruffini – that he has no right to something he hasn't slaved over and loved all his life.'

'So, the irresistible force – Sir Frank – meets the immovable object – the Ruffinis! Well, until someone tells me to stop I shall go on doing what I'm here for.' Bertrand glanced at Nell and

then went on more hesitantly. 'I don't envy your husband *his* job.
He must know what the legal system is like here – it would
probably take years for a challenge to Ruffini to come to court.'
Bertrand waved that subject aside and embarked on a different
one.

'I find this stay here fascinating – the more so because the
member of the party who seemed most unhappy at the beginning of it – Lady Middleton – is the one who is now thoroughly
enjoying herself! I think she has you to thank for that.'

Nell smiled but shook her head. 'I persuaded her to have her
hair cut. Friendship with the Count has done the rest – he makes
her feel of value.'

Bertrand suddenly lifted Nell's hand to his lips, then returned
it gently to her lap. 'I hope *you* feel valued – you should do.'
Then he stood up and smiled ruefully at her. '*Mes hommages,
madame – c'est tout ce que je peux dire, malheureusement.*'

A moment later he'd walked away, leaving her uncomfortably
aware that one more complication had been added to the
emotional turmoil they were already in.

She hadn't come to terms with that discovery when her next
visitor appeared, but Joan Middleton hesitated at the sight of the
pencil in her hand.

'I'm interrupting – you want to get on with your story.'

Nell laid the pencil down again. 'The story can wait – inspir-
ation was lacking anyway. I thought you were with the others at
the pool.'

Joan shook her head. 'First of all I went to see Vittorio – I
guessed he'd be feeling to blame for what has happened. He
thinks that if he'd known the Ruffinis better, he'd have understood their feelings about the farm, instead of just assuming that
they were only waiting for the chance to leave, like the other
tenants.'

'"First of all", you said,' Nell commented. 'Then what
happened?'

'I talked to Frank – asked him to reassure Vittorio that *no*
blame attaches to him.'

As fascinated now as Bertrand had been by this once demor-
alized wife, Nell smiled warmly at her. 'I can't wait to hear what
he said.'

Joan looked glad to be able to praise her husband. 'He's never petty, you know; he agreed that he'd known all along there was a tenant at one of the farms that the Count wouldn't evict. And, in a funny sort of way, I think he's rather pleased that there's something his money can't buy! He's going to tell Vittorio that.'

'"Curiouser and curiouser",' Nell quoted. 'That will teach me not to reckon that I can guess how people will behave. But what happens now about the hotel?'

'I don't know – I left him talking with Giles about that.' She smiled ruefully at Nell. 'Poor Giles *and* you – so much for the holiday you were going to take. I wish Frank had never started on this hotel idea, but I can't see him giving it up – he doesn't work like that.'

'Well, we can't hope that he'll change to that extent, and Giles doesn't like giving up either; it's probably why they get on so well,' Nell admitted. She picked up her pencil as a gentle hint that the conversation could end there. With her new-found confidence, Joan might next turn to the subject of Jacqueline, and this was something Nell couldn't bear to discuss with anyone else.

'You deserve a siesta after all today's good work,' she said instead, and her companion blushed and agreed.

Left alone once more, Nell abandoned any pretence of working; there was too much else to think about. But, rather than be still further waylaid, she abandoned the garden as well, went indoors, and tucked herself up on her seat at the bedroom window.

The day had been too eventful already, but it had one more surprise to spring. Carlotta knocked at the door to call her to the telephone, and she heard her brother's voice at the other end of the line.

'You sound odd – are you all right?' she asked quickly.

'I'm in a hotel room – in Milan!' he shouted. 'And there's a lot of traffic outside. I'm not very useful at the Garden at the moment, but someone remembered that I speak Italian; so I got the lovely job of conferring with colleagues at La Scala – we're doing a joint production of *Don Carlos* next season. But I'm officially on sick leave still, so I thought I'd nip down and hang round for a bit – in Florence maybe, if you don't want me too close.'

'You can hang around here,' Nell suggested. 'There's plenty of room, and I'm quite sure that Lady Middleton would make you welcome. Let me know when your train will get to Florence and we'll be there to pick you up.'

'You sound tired,' Jonathan said. 'Is the great man too much at close quarters?'

'Not really, but there's a lot to tell you, and I shall be glad to see my little brother.'

'Well, tapping out a report with one hand is slow work, but I'll finish it tonight and catch the first train I can after breakfast. I'm quite keen to see how the filthy rich live! *A domani*, Nell.'

She put down the receiver, smiling at the thought that he was at least as near as Milan. It was a gift from heaven that he should be there so unexpectedly, and she got ready for dinner feeling that an exhausting day had finally redeemed itself.

# Twelve

Jonathan's suggestion of finding a hotel in Florence was firmly vetoed.

'On his own there, with an arm in plaster?' Joan Middleton sounded horrified. 'Nell, of course he must come here and be looked after.'

His sister smiled gratefully, not pointing out that, with or without the use of both arms, Jonathan was able to manage very nicely. A handsome face and appealing ways seemed to make life's doors open for him very obligingly. Instead, she went in search of Beppe to ask whether a lift into Florence the following day would conflict with his other duties. Knowing that a true-born Italian male liked nothing better than to be at the wheel of a car, she got the answer she expected, and went back to the *salone* smiling at the sheer helpfulness of the Count's servants.

Lady Middleton announced the news of Jonathan's visit as soon as the others came into the room, and it was apparent to Nell that Giles looked relieved. Anything that diverted her attention from Jacqueline was welcome at the moment, and it would help bridge the awkwardness they both now felt in sharing a room – there would be something else to talk about besides themselves.

'I'll drive you to the station tomorrow,' Giles suggested when they were alone, but Nell shook her head.

'I'm sure you've got work to do, and in any case I can't disappoint Beppe now. He truly loves Vittorio's *machina* and can't understand why his dear *padrone* never seems to want to use it.'

Giles grinned, suddenly looking less careworn. 'The Count is the least typical Italian I've met. I doubt if he knows the "beautiful game" even exists, though it's almost a religion with his countrymen!' Then Giles's voice changed. 'I'm glad Jonathan is coming, Nell. It isn't Frank's fault that this visit is turning out to be no holiday at all, but . . .' He hesitated, uncertain how to go on, and didn't mind being interrupted.

'What happens next about the hotel?'

'We make Sergio a final offer. If he refuses, I suppose we look for another site. The land Frank now owns was only meant to become the hotel grounds and golf course.'

'So what will he do with it now?'

'Try to sell it again – what else?'

Nell nodded, and there the subject rested.

The following morning, with Jonathan's train not due until mid-afternoon, she went to mass in Poggione. Walking out at the end of the service, she heard her name and, when she turned round, found Marco Ruffini standing there.

'May I offer you some coffee?' he suggested. 'My grandfather says that I was rude when you came to Pratolino. I'm sorry if that was so.'

It was a reluctant apology, but Nell was more interested in the discovery that this communist-leaning relative was also, it seemed, an active Catholic. She smilingly agreed that coffee would be welcome, and they crossed the piazza together to one of the café's pavement tables.

When the coffee had been brought, she waited for him to begin the conversation while she watched the swirl of milk froth in her cup. He could look at her unobserved for a moment. She was different from the young women he was used to. Not beautiful, she was nevertheless attractive, even though he'd made up his mind to disapprove of someone who belonged with the people at the Villa Guidi.

'I suppose your husband was angry when you went back to the villa,' he said suddenly. 'He shouldn't have asked you to come.'

'He didn't,' Nell answered. 'Sir Frank Middleton wanted me to assure you that both Count Vittorio and I consider your grand-father the proper owner of Pratolino.'

Marco nodded; that at least was right. 'So *he* was angry that he can't buy the farm?'

'Well, certainly disappointed,' Nell agreed, improvising a little. 'He'd already acquired the farms adjoining yours.'

'What will he do now – build his hotel there?'

'Apparently not; but I'm not the person to ask about this. You should speak to my husband or to Sir Frank himself.'

Marco was silent for a minute or two – like the Count, another untypical Italian, she thought. Then he decided to explain. 'I should only tell them what they ought to be able to see for themselves: that it's wrong to cover good land with buildings. My grandfather and I could make proper use of those farms, but we should never be able to afford to buy them.' He looked across the table at Nell, and an unexpected smile changed his face. 'Was I rude? If so, I am sorry – it was no way to treat a sort of cousin.'

'The "sort of cousin" forgives you,' she said gently. 'I'm still glad to have met you and your grandfather, and it's meant a lot to me to discover where my darling Francesca grew up.'

Marco nodded again, then put money on the table for their coffee. 'I'm on my way to Pontassieve but I could take you back to the villa first.'

Nell shook her head. 'Thank you, but I shall enjoy the walk. By the way, another member of the family arrives this afternoon – my brother Jonathan. I'd like you to meet him as well.'

Marco thought about this for a moment. 'You could bring him to Pratolino. We don't visit Villa Guidi.' Then he made her a little bow. '*Arrivederci*, cousin Nell.'

When his jeep had turned the corner of the square, she started on her return journey, but almost immediately stopped again to consider what had just come into her mind. Then she shook her head and went on walking, but after another hundred yards she stopped again. *Why not?* her mind asked. Nothing would probably come of it, but nothing would come of nothing, as King Lear had rightly said. *All right*, she said to her mind; *I'll try it, if I can only work out how it can be done.*

The train from Milan arrived on time to the minute and, waiting at the barrier, Nell could easily make out Jonathan's fair head above the people around him. It was no surprise that he was being shepherded by a motherly woman who'd shanghaied another passenger into carrying his luggage. Nell and Jonathan parted company with them in a flurry of thanks, and she led him outside to where Beppe stood guarding the car.

When they were settled inside, she said, in Italian so as not to exclude Beppe from the conversation, that her news could wait until they reached the villa, so Jonathan entertained them all the way to Poggione with a racy account of backstage Milanese life.

Only when he'd been welcomed by his hostess, advised by Lucia to rest after a long journey, and eyed approvingly by Carlotta, was Nell able to tell him in the privacy of his bedroom what had been happening since she arrived in Tuscany.

'I can't believe I arrived eight days ago,' she finished up. 'It feels more like eight weeks.'

'It's some house party,' Jonathan said consideringly. 'Thwarted tycoon, browbeaten wife, poisonous daughter, and a very odd French couple, to say nothing of the invisible owner of this sumptuous place. What a mercy they have us – you, me and Giles – to spread a little sweetness and light.' Then he added casually, 'Or isn't Giles adding much in that direction?'

As usual, her brother had sensed what she'd left unsaid, but she merely replied that, like her husband, he might find Jacqueline Middleton anything but poisonous. It was easier to talk about their relatives at the farm.

'Marco gave me permission to take you to meet his grand-father, but you'll have to try not to be too operatic! Sergio admits that his grandson is an avowed communist. That being so, Marco is bound to disapprove of you, pandering to the decadent tastes of the idle rich.'

'I shall be nothing if not manly and serious,' Jonathan said solemnly. 'I might even ask an intelligent question about what *he* does for a living.' Then his voice changed. 'The Ruffinis *are* bucking the trend, though, aren't they? From what I hear, no one wants to stay in farming, and Tuscany is becoming a theme park, just like Venice.'

'Mostly true,' Nell agreed, 'but not at Pratolino. Frank Middleton has found himself up against people still devoted to their land.' Then she smiled at her brother. 'Lucia's advice was good – a nap before dinner; you look tired.'

He looked at the snowy bedlinen and heaped pillows. 'It's a thought,' he admitted. 'I finished my report at three o'clock this morning.'

'Dinner's not till eight. Dress informal, but we make a little effort, so I hope you've brought something more than jeans and tee-shirts.'

'Fear not; I shall do you proud,' he answered and, as usual with Jonathan, she realized that a laughing comment meant more than it seemed to say. She was reminded of something else he'd said.

'You weren't quite right about the house party: the Count is no longer invisible – you'll meet him this evening – and Joan Middleton can't be described as browbeaten any more. It's the best thing that's happened here, seeing her come to life.' Then she blew Jonathan a kiss and left the room.

His arrival made a difference that evening. Sylvie showed signs of monopolizing a guest with whom, as she said, she felt such rapport; and Jacqueline, never inclined to be sidelined, exerted herself to be more provocative than usual with the newcomer. Jonathan very properly attended to his host and hostess, and enjoyed talking to the Count, who confessed to being a regular visitor to La Scala in Milan. Balked, Jacqueline returned her attention to Giles, but Nell wondered what he made of her blatant attack on another man.

The following morning, after her Italian lesson with Joan, Nell offered her brother a visit to the farm.

'You'll like Sergio, I think,' she said as they walked along the track. 'Marco's a harder nut to crack, but he's well worth knowing.'

This time her knock at the farmhouse door was answered by a small, round woman who could have been Lucia's sister. She proudly showed them into the *salone*, a room that was clearly never used, and then bustled away to find the *padrone*. He arrived a moment or two later to find them studying a silver-framed photograph on a side table. A young Francesca smiled at them, her brother beside her, and also in the picture were a smaller boy, who was presumably Sergio himself, and a tall young man, whom Nell guessed to be their grandfather – the English officer who had become part of the family for a little while.

'Forgive us, please,' Nell said to Sergio, 'we hadn't seen that before. This is my brother, Jonathan Ashley, who also speaks Italian.'

The two men shook hands, and then Sergio looked round the room. 'I don't know why Assunta brought you in here. Let's go outside – Marco is there as well.'

He led them to a vine-shaded terrace at the back of the house, where his grandson sat splicing a new handle on a pruning-knife. Sergio introduced him to Jonathan, then pointed to the visitor's plastered arm.

'You've hurt yourself.'

'An accident – it's mending now, but it gives me an excuse to come and visit Nell.' Jonathan's charming smile appeared. 'I gather we're distant cousins! It's nice to know, because Nell and I are rather short of relatives!'

Marco's reticent face began to relax into friendliness, and Sergio was already beaming.

Now Nell joined in. 'I've told Jonathan that you intend to produce better and better wine and olive oil.'

Sergio nodded. 'We're doing all we can, but each small improvement costs time and money. We need more space too, for Marco's grafting experiments and the new vines he wants to try.'

Nell felt her way carefully now. 'It seems to me that you work very hard already. Wouldn't more land mean more work than you can manage?'

Marco answered for his grandfather. 'There's help available as soon as we can afford it. I know families who moved away but now find they hate city life. They'd come back given the chance.'

He sounded sure enough for Nell to believe him; then, as Sergio bustled indoors, his grave face broke into a smile. 'A mid-morning glass of wine is my grandfather's habit, but today he'll want you to taste a Ruffini vintage that we're proud of!'

It was delicious when Sergio returned with it – delicately straw-coloured, pleasantly dry without being acidic. Sipping it, Jonathan pronounced it perfect for pre-lunch drinking on a summer's day. 'You'd find a ready market for it in England, if you can produce enough of it,' he suggested.

'We can't yet,' Marco answered. 'There are still old vines to be grubbed up and replaced . . . always more work to be done – like now!' He drank what had been poured for him and then explained that the morning's task had to be resumed – the spraying of the vines with copper-sulphate solution to prevent disease; arduous work with a small tank of it strapped to his back.

Sergio watched him go, then spoke sadly to Nell. 'You were right – he works too hard, and I'm not as useful as I once was. But what he does he loves – it shows, I think.'

'It certainly does,' she said at once, 'but I hope there's a little leisure – time left for friends, perhaps for finding a girl to share life with.'

Sergio shook his head. 'His friends are the people he occasionally sees at political meetings – good citizens, of course, but always so serious! I'd like him to enjoy still being young.'

Nell hesitated before asking her next question. 'Marco said that you and he don't go to the Villa Guidi. Would you break the rule if Lady Middleton invited you? Count Guidi doesn't have to be there, but he's a very nice man, and he *is* your nearest neighbour.'

Sergio's smile was suddenly full of understanding. 'You think it's time we grew up – buried the past and became friends! If the lady's husband agreed to the invitation, I would come myself, but I can't answer for Marco – most likely not, I think.'

Nell privately thought so too, but instead of saying so she thanked Sergio for letting them come, and they said their goodbyes.

'Nice man,' Jonathan remarked as they climbed the track again. 'Thank God the Count isn't minded to fight him for ownership of the place – he clearly loves every inch of it.'

'Marco, too,' Nell agreed.

Jonathan turned to look at her. 'Did I detect some hidden agenda in that "more land, more work" question?'

'Marco needs more land and more capital; Frank Middleton has both. What are the chances of getting him interested in an investment, do you think?'

As requested, Jonathan thought. 'Probably nil,' he finally replied. 'Middleton is no fairy godfather, and he has no reason to want to help the Ruffinis.'

'That's what I think too,' Nell admitted sadly, and they walked the rest of the way in silence.

# Thirteen

Lunch over, Giles prepared for another assault on estate agents with land to sell. He accepted gratefully when Jonathan offered to go with him and act as interpreter. Nell waited for what she thought would come next and saw Jacqueline quickly leave the room. Back a few minutes later, her lunchtime shorts and shirt had been replaced by a slightly more businesslike, sleeveless dress. She smiled at Jonathan.

'Giles always gets me as well – lucky man!'

The lucky man made haste to explain. 'Frank is under orders to rest here, and Jacqueline doesn't quite trust me to do the best I can for her father. Added to that, she's a first-rate driver.'

But the glance they exchanged wasn't lost on Jonathan, and he felt Nell's hurt as if it was his own. She must know for sure now what she'd only hinted before. He was more than ready to help, but how? His own all-out assault on Jacqueline might work – she was a siren who waited for the approach of any personable male, but she was clearly smitten with Giles, and Nell would be doubly hurt by what would seem his own treachery. Better, perhaps, just to irritate a girl who'd find it hard to accept his failure to find her irresistible.

At last he broke the silence left by what Giles had said. 'Let the signorina drive by all means, as long as she doesn't keep talking – girls do as a rule, don't you find?' Then, before she could draw breath to reply, he waved a cheerful goodbye to Nell and left the room.

Giles and Jacqueline followed him out, leaving her torn by his clear intention to do battle on her behalf. She was touched, but well aware that he would thereby add another tension to life at the villa. It only needed Frank Middleton to suspect his wife of falling in love with Vittorio Guidi for the emotional tangle to be complete.

Joan waited until Frank had left for the siesta he took under duress each afternoon, then smiled ruefully at Nell.

'Poor man – he hates inactivity of any kind, and it's being forced on him here in more ways than one!'

Nell hesitated, then decided to take the plunge. 'Perhaps what I'm about to ask will make things worse – you must refuse if so.'

Her friend looked merely puzzled. 'Why should I refuse? Just tell me what you want.'

Nell began to explain. 'You know how things are between Sir Frank and the Ruffinis, and between them and the Count – complicated to say the least. But, if it can possibly be arranged, I want them to meet. If you were willing to invite them here, Marco might not come, but I think that at least his grandfather would.'

Joan smiled at her across the table. 'Do I get to know why you want them here?'

'Not yet, if you don't mind,' Nell said regretfully. 'You'd have to sell the idea to Sir Frank on the grounds of good-neighbourliness, and it might be easier if you truly didn't know about my ulterior motive!' She saw faint alarm in Joan's face and shook her head. 'It's nothing to worry about. Jonathan would tell you that I always mean well and rarely do any harm.'

'And Vittorio?' Joan asked. 'Is he to be included as well?'

'I think so. It's high time the griefs of the past were buried here. But refuse if you want to.'

'Of course I shan't refuse!' Joan thought for a moment, then shook her head. 'Good-neighbourliness won't impress my husband at all. I shall simply say that we owe your relatives the civility of a dinner invitation.'

Nell smiled at her affectionately, still marvelling at a change that had been only for the good. It seemed more than likely that the suggestion, however presented, would be vetoed; but the following morning she was instructed to ring Sergio and give him Lady Middleton's invitation. At the same time Nell urged him to persuade Marco to come, using the same useful weapon of civility. It would be a slight to Francesca's grandchildren if he sat on his communist high-horse and stayed at home. Sergio thoughtfully agreed with this, and the following evening both he and Marco walked up from the farm and crossed the threshold of the Villa Guidi for the first time in their lives.

Tense with anticipation, Nell had imagined everything that might go wrong: Jacqueline patronizing guests she saw as mere Tuscan yokels, Sergio resenting the Count's generosity in waiving any claim to Pratolino, Middleton trying to bully him into selling after all, and Marco antagonizing everyone by openly disapproving of new-found wealth as much as age-old privilege.

That none of this seemed to be happening owed much to Joan Middleton's tact and kindness. But also, as Nell had hoped, her husband *was* impressed with Marco – recognizing qualities he prized: acumen, single-mindedness and a passion for working hard. It was only when they were drinking coffee and brandy after dinner that awkwardness crept in – thanks, inevitably, to Jacqueline. Bored with the conversations going on, she wandered to the far end of the room, selected music for the player, and then beckoned to Giles to go and dance with her. Embarrassed but obedient, he left the others and went to join her.

Nell thought her intention couldn't have been more clear: the others present were to understand who it was she chose to single out. What Giles himself thought about it Nell could no longer guess. The least vain of men, he'd never even seemed to notice his attractiveness to women, but that had been *then*; she didn't know about *now*. As she thought about it, she became aware of the conversation their host had started with Marco, who spoke more English than his grandfather.

'We have a saying where I come from – "Why flog a dead horse?"' To further make his point, Frank Middleton pointed a finger at Marco. 'Farming's finished here, but you could make a name for yourself easily enough doing something else.'

Marco's stern young face stared back at him. 'Farming *isn't* finished – how can it be when people still need to eat? Growing food is what we should be doing here, not making a holiday place of Tuscany for rich men.'

'You're listening to an enthusiast, Sir Frank,' Nell hurriedly put in. 'Marco is committed to what he does.'

'He's committed to thinking it's a crime to make money, apparently!' Middleton turned again to Marco. 'Let me remind you, my dear young enthusiast, that most rich men I know have laboured hard and long for what they now possess. They're in need of a holiday occasionally, and if they can be persuaded to come here, they'll bring their money with them.'

'We don't want them here,' Marco insisted. 'A large part of Italy is mountainous, unworkable. Let them go there if they must have a playground.'

Seeing Middleton's mouth tighten, Count Vittorio took it upon himself to draw the enemy fire. 'It's true, Sir Frank – good agricultural land is very limited; you mustn't blame Marco for not wanting it wasted on golf courses!'

'I take the point,' his host conceded stiffly, 'but not many rich men have had the time to become mountaineers. They'll choose to go elsewhere to spend the wealth that this part of Tuscany could do with.' Then again he returned to Marco. 'And there's another thing, lad: however hard you work, you're limited by what your grandfather's land can produce. Today's brutal economics don't favour small-scale farming.'

A respectful silence followed this pronouncement, broken at last by Nell. Heart in mouth and voice huskier than usual, she tried to sound confident. 'You're right, Sir Frank. Marco needs more land for all his schemes – land adjoining what his grandfather owns. If you have no use for it now, could this be one of the investment opportunities Giles says you're so brilliant at seizing?'

Aware now of the purpose of the dinner party, his answering smile was as genial as a sword-thrust. 'You've forgotten something, I'm afraid. I'm an international entrepreneur, not a bloody do-gooder, or a gambler on forlorn hopes!' Then, to Marco, he went on, 'Forgive the plain speaking, but I like people to know where I stand. You may not relish the idea, but tourism is the future here – look at Venice, Siena, Florence itself. Put your heart and soul into that and you'll prosper. Work your small plot until you drop and you'll still end up poor and broken-hearted.'

It ended the discussion and also the dinner party. By standing up to bow over Joan's hand, the Count made it easy for the Ruffinis to follow suit and say goodnight. They left a silence behind that no one seemed eager to break. At last, Nell moved to one of the long, open windows and stepped out thankfully to the terrace and the warm, still night. Then she became aware that Bertrand had followed her. Coming to stand beside her, he pointed at the star-scattered sky.

'Look up there, Nell,' he suggested, 'and don't fret too much because your plan didn't work.'

'Was it that obvious?' she asked quietly. 'I meant to wait . . . just let Sir Frank meet Sergio and Marco. It's what I *should* have done. All I've achieved is to make Sir Frank suspicious and Marco feel humiliated. I told Joan beforehand that I don't do any harm. What a lie *that* was!'

Bertrand laid a hand on her arm. 'Don't you have a saying about angels rushing in where fools fear to tread?'

She smiled ruefully at him. 'I'm sure you know you've got it the wrong way round, but I give you full marks for kindness!' Struck by the strangeness of this conversation with another man while her husband danced with Jacqueline, she suddenly wanted Bertrand to know that she now valued him properly. 'You like to wear a sophisticated disguise, but underneath you're a very kind and perceptive man; I'm glad I've come to realize that.' But the conversation had become too personal and, afraid of what he might say next, she hurried on.

'It wasn't a stupid idea, even though I ruined it. Sir Frank *should* have been impressed by Marco, thought him worth helping.'

'Marco ruined it all by himself,' Bertrand said firmly. 'The great man *was* impressed; he just didn't like being judged and found wanting by someone half his age. He probably made the same mistake himself when he was as young as Marco is.'

'Then I shall take comfort from that,' Nell said wryly. She turned to glance into the room behind them. The dancing was now over, and Giles and Jacqueline were deep in conversation with her father. The others seemed to have retired to bed.

'Three sensible people at least,' Nell said with a tired smile. 'I think I'll follow their example when I've thanked Lucia for a lovely meal.'

Bertrand watched her walk towards the kitchen quarters and then stepped back into the *salone* himself in time to hear what Jacqueline had to say about the evening's guests.

'I don't know why we had to have them here at all – they're little more than peasants, and red peasants at that.'

Bertrand opened his mouth to protest, but Giles was ahead of him, speaking with unusual firmness. 'My dear, that's *not* what they are. Say the Ruffinis have proved a maddening stumbling block and I'd agree with you, but Sergio and his grandson are intelligent, educated people, and they're entitled to whatever political colour they choose.'

She didn't like being reproved but managed a pouting smile.

'What's more, they're related to your wife – you feel you have to stick up for them. But at least admit that Marco Ruffini is a boring killjoy!'

Giles's smile answered her. 'I'll admit that it's hard to warm to anyone quite as seriously inclined as he is.'

Tired of this discussion, Middleton brought them back to the matter in hand. 'Let's forget the Ruffinis, shall we? If we haven't got an alternative site a week from today, we give up trying to put this bit of Tuscany on the map, and the Count can have his villa back. I don't say it isn't beautiful, but we can't help people who won't help themselves. And what's more, I'm getting sick of endless blue skies and Lucia's pasta for lunch every day.'

Sir Frank was homesick for Huddersfield, Giles suddenly realized – wanted clouds and black pudding and the sound in his ears of his own countrymen. The dream he'd started with might have to be written off as one of his rare failures; he'd accept it and move on, unchanged by this Tuscan interlude. But it might not be so easy for the rest of them, all of them changed in different ways by what had happened.

Giles remembered what Nell had said in London before they started out: Frank Middleton changed people. But it was unfair to blame him now – it was something in this ancient Etruscan place that had made the alterations they were caught in.

# Fourteen

Nell was apparently fast asleep when Giles went upstairs. Closed eyes meant nothing, of course, but he accepted the pretence, knowing that it was all he could do for her at the moment. But the following morning, when she came back into the bedroom showered and dressed for her usual early morning visit to the garden, he was waiting to talk to her.

'Nell, about last night—'

It was as far as he got before she interrupted him. 'Last night was my fault. I asked Joan to invite Sergio and Marco. The visit seemed to be going rather well until I spoiled it by speaking out of turn.'

Her confession deflected Giles from the apology he'd been about to make. 'Was that the purpose of the invitation – to get Frank interested in Pratolino?'

Nell nodded, then explained. 'It seemed a beautifully simple solution to two problems: Marco needs more land, Frank has land to get rid of. I hoped he wouldn't be able to resist it. Instead, he used his sledgehammer-to-crack-a-nut technique and tried to humiliate Marco. A gracious refusal doesn't seem to enter his head.'

'It isn't common in the business jungle he inhabits,' Giles pointed out. Then he considered what else Nell had said. 'Two things were wrong last night. The solution wasn't one that Frank had thought of himself, and Marco seemed determined to alienate the very man who could help him. I'd say the failure wasn't yours at all.'

She admitted that Bertrand had said the same thing, and registered Giles's change of expression. 'We talked on the terrace for a while after Sergio and Marco had gone home. You wouldn't have noticed – you were otherwise engaged with Jacqueline.' She managed to say it evenly, but a faint flush touched his cheekbones.

'I'm sorry, Nell.' The apology sounded stiffer than he meant to, and he tried again. 'Jacqueline was feeling left out, that's all.'

There was no response from his wife, and he abruptly changed the subject.

'Frank issued an ultimatum last night. He's allowing me a week to find another site; after that he'll give up. He's tired of trying to deal with people whose mentality he doesn't understand and who don't seem to appreciate what he's offering them.'

'Well, it *is* their choice,' Nell insisted gently. 'What happens if you can't find a site?'

'We pay off Bertrand and Sylvie, hand the Count back his villa, and go home – mission not accomplished.'

Giles would see it, Nell knew, as *his* failure, whether Frank Middleton did or not, but, sorry as she felt about it, she couldn't spare him her next question. 'What exactly do *we* go home to?' The briefness of it told him how hard it was for her to ask, when their whole future life depended on it.

He came to stand beside her at the open window, and for a moment they could have been any carefree couple content to share the sweet morning air and watch the garden below them waking to another day. Then he tried to answer her question.

'Frank still wants me to join him – run his London office while he stays in Huddersfield. I do want the job, Nell; it's a challenge that knocks anything Marchants can offer me into a cocked hat. But something tells me I can't have you *and* the job, even though Jacqueline would be in Huddersfield with her father. Am I right?'

'I'm afraid you're not right about *her*,' Nell said sadly. 'You must already know what Joan has told me about Jacqueline's real mother – Huddersfield wasn't enough for her, and nor will it be for her daughter. She wants a high-flying life in London with you, and she's abetted by her father who wants the pair of you to carry on his empire. If you can see where I fit into that scenario, I'm afraid I can't.'

He put his hands on her shoulders and turned her to face him. 'My dear, this is fantasy – I'm to be Frank's man in London, not his son-in-law.' What he had to say next was more difficult, but he did his best. 'Which brings us to Jacqueline. I agree that she wants life in London, and for the moment she might see it as including me, but that won't last. I'm fifteen years older than she is, and she's intelligent enough to know that propinquity and animal lust aren't the basis to build her future on. She'll leave me behind as soon as it suits her.'

'And where will that leave you?' Nell asked.

'Sane again, I hope, and ashamed of the pain I've caused you.' His hand gently brushed back her hair. 'I know I said this once before, but can you wait to see how things work out in London? If not, I must give up Frank's job.'

It meant that, in reality, she had no choice at all. He couldn't – or wouldn't – see what the Middletons wanted of him, but to ask him to cut himself loose would mean the end of their marriage anyway. She knew what success – now embodied in Frank Middleton – meant to him; knew that only success would seem to justify his parents' desperate struggle to send him to Shrewsbury School and Cambridge.

She nodded in answer to his question and saw him smile for the breathing space he'd been given. Now they could talk of something else.

'With time so short, we have to split our forces. I'm going to ask Jonathan to interpret for Jacqueline, and it would be nice if you'd come with me.'

It was so obvious a reward for good behaviour that she was hard put to it to answer quietly, instead of shouting at him. 'I'm afraid I must do something else – go and apologize to Sergio and Marco for the mistake I made in bringing them here. Let it be a lesson to me not to interfere in other people's lives in future.'

This time she was given a smile that was real and gentle. 'What you call interference hasn't done all that badly – Joan is a changed woman, Vittorio Guidi's no longer a hermit, Bertrand has become likeable, and even Sylvie shows signs of being human. I wouldn't put it past you to teach Frank "gracious refusals" before you're done!'

'You jest, of course,' Nell said solemnly; then, assuming that this conversation was over, she started to leave the room.

His voice halted her. 'Nell, your beautiful solution – was it just a shot in the dark or something more reasonable than that?'

'It seemed reasonable enough to me,' she answered slowly. 'Given what he needs – more land and more working capital – Marco *will* succeed in producing the best wine and olive oil in Tuscany. And if Frank Middleton really wants to bring prosperity here, why doesn't he help a young man who belongs to this place and is dedicated, heart and soul, to what he's doing?'

Her husband's expression didn't tell her whether he thought this sufficiently reasonable or not, but, either way, she'd said all she could on the subject.

'I'll see you at breakfast,' she suggested instead. 'I've some friends to say hello to in the garden.'

Curious about them, he watched from the window as she emerged from the house and crossed the terrace, but the green jungle beyond swallowed her up and he was no wiser about her friends until the sketchbook she'd left on the table caught his eye. Leafing through it, he met the boy on the dolphin, the little running fawn and a host of other small animals, real or imaginary, who inhabited her magic garden. He knew it was how she worked – here were the characters whose story she would weave. At least what he was looking at meant that she would salvage something from these unhappy weeks. But the drawings were enchanting in themselves, and he put the book down, unhappily aware of how often in the past he'd heard himself explain to friends that his wife just amused herself by creating books for children.

When breakfast was over, he announced that, in order to save precious time, they must now split up and search in different directions for the site Frank needed. Before Jacqueline could open her mouth to protest, he smilingly added that his brother-in-law had been prevailed upon to go with her, while he himself went alone. Jonathan's resigned expression was all the added challenge she needed. With a taunting smile at him, she promised not to drive faster than his frail nerves could bear.

'There's also the little matter of not talking,' he said anxiously. 'You haven't forgotten that?'

With slightly gritted teeth now, she assured him that they could spend the entire day not exchanging a word, and, on this understanding, Giles watched them set out, not knowing which of them to feel sorry for. Jacqueline had weapons not available to her passenger, but Jonathan loved his sister, and he was adept at dealing with tantrums in his professional life.

Silence did indeed reign in the car until they were halfway to

Arezzo. Then Jonathan, who was map-reading, had to warn the driver to return to the speed limit – something she hadn't so far observed – because they were approaching the turn-off they needed. Jacqueline looked at the landscape around them – the higher foothills of the mountains that made up the long rocky spine of Italy – and predicted that Giles had sent them on a wild-goose chase.

'Look at it,' she demanded, removing one hand from the steering wheel to point to what was outside the window. 'Who'd be mad enough to build a luxury hotel here?'

'Given the gradients, a golf course might be difficult,' Jonathan conceded. 'But the scenery is magnificent, and not every world-weary tycoon wants to spend his off-duty time banging a small ball about.'

'You're acquainted with these people, of course,' Jacqueline commented; 'know exactly what they might want instead?'

Jonathan didn't mind the insinuation. 'Apart from your father, I don't know a single one. I'm merely assuming that some of them at least have the sense to spend their time more profitably.'

'Profitably as in listening to opera, for example – watching an overweight heroine, supposedly dying of consumption, sit up to belt out her last-act aria? Where's the sense in that?'

'Today's divas are *not* overweight,' Jonathan said firmly. 'Most of them are built like racehorses. I concede that opera badly performed is ludicrous; on a good night, however, it's an unbeatable synthesis of all the arts – musical, dramatic and visual. If you can't accept that simple, incontrovertible fact, then you're no better than a cultural moron.'

He was about to throw in a slighting reference to Huddersfield as well, then remembered that he'd never been there: moreover, she *was* still in charge of the car. Instead, he pointed out that they were now approaching what they'd come to inspect.

An hour later they drove away again after a difficult interview with the frail, elderly owner of a once-beautiful, now crumbling *castello* whose estate boundary unfortunately nudged a very new, very ugly housing estate.

'Well, say something!' Jacqueline exploded. 'Don't just sit there. At least say it was a completely wasted visit.'

She sounded angry, but he couldn't guess who with – Giles

for sending them there, the estate agent for concealing the truth, or the Countess herself for being unaware of the hopeless white elephant she was desperate to sell.

'I was about to say that I'll buy you a drink at the first bar we come to – we need it,' Jonathan remarked. 'I don't like this job; Giles can count me out of it from now on.'

Now her anger switched to him. 'The harsh realities of life too much for such a delicate flower? That's what comes of living in your make-believe world. You should go outside the opera house occasionally.'

'I occasionally do,' he pointed out. 'The down-and-outs' shelter where I lend a hand is quite real enough for me.'

Silenced, she returned her attention to the road until Jonathan spotted a pleasant-looking trattoria in the little piazza they were driving into. 'There . . . that will do and, since it's lunchtime, I'll even buy you some good food as well.'

She pulled up and followed him out to a shady pavement table. Then, with their orders taken and a flagon of chilled white wine in front of them, she suddenly opened fire.

'You don't like me, do you? I'm the rich man's spoiled brat of a daughter, brought up to think she can have whatever she happens to want.'

Jonathan poured wine into her glass before he answered. 'It's roughly what I'm thinking,' he agreed with a faint smile. 'In the normal course of events that wouldn't worry me, but it does when what you seem to want is my sister's husband.'

The frontal attack took her a moment to recover from, but she managed her usual careless shrug. 'Wanting would do me no good if Giles was still attached to his wife.' Confidence returning, she smiled at him across the table. 'You've a very old-fashioned idea of matrimony. In today's world, a woman who can no longer satisfy her husband must expect to lose him to someone who can. It works the other way round too, of course; I'm all for equality!'

They were interrupted by the waiter bringing their food, and Jonathan watched him walk away dazzled by the smile she'd given him. Dark, shining hair, tanned skin and perfectly proportioned body drew the eye of every man there, and how well she knew it. He was put in mind of a pedigree cat – the same sinuous

grace, intelligence and total self-concern. But he put the comparison aside to answer her.

'Nell and Giles were married in accordance with the service
in the Book of Common Prayer, thereby promising to live together
in holy love until their lives' end. Such a promise doesn't matter
to you?'

'Like I said – old-fashioned,' she commented. 'But you might
give me credit for thinking of Giles as well as myself. He's ambitious and he wants what's being offered to him.'

It was probably true, Jonathan reflected ruefully, but he tried
to match her confidence. 'Yes, he's ambitious, but only up to a
point, and at that point your argument breaks down, because he
does still love his wife – what man wouldn't? So my money is
on their promises being kept. Disappointing for you, of course,
but even the rich man's daughter must accept a failure now and
then.'

'Well, we'll have to wait and see,' Jacqueline suggested. Then
her slow, enticing smile reappeared. 'I give you marks for sticking
up for your sister, but I'm afraid you're a rotten gambler, Jonathan
Ashley!'

'The Italians have a phrase for it – "what will be, will be",'
Jonathan replied. 'Let's leave it at that, shall we? We'll finish our
lunch, then go back and report to your father, who will not be
very pleased with us for a totally wasted journey.'

# Fifteen

Once both search parties had left that morning, followed by Bertrand and Sylvie bent on some exploration of their own, the usual pattern of the day had begun – Frank Middleton in his office, checking overnight events around the globe; Nell and Joan settling down to their enjoyable Italian lesson.

But the villa's normal peaceful routine was suddenly shattered by a commotion in the kitchen. Then a white-faced Beppe ran out to them on the terrace to announce that Carlotta, chopping vegetables in the kitchen, had cut her hand badly. The gash was found to be deep and bleeding so freely that Lady Middleton insisted on a visit to the local surgery. Makeshift dressing in place, Carlotta was driven to Poggione by her father, with Nell beside her, holding her uninjured hand for comfort.

Half an hour later, with the wound cleaned and stitched, she was ready to be taken home again; Nell stayed behind to buy what Lucia needed for the day.

The shopping was soon done but, instead of going straight back to the villa, she took the opportunity to call at the *presbiterio* and enquire after old Luciano Pavese. This time the housekeeper assured her that he would welcome a visit. If the signora would only let herself out into the cloister by the vestry door, she would find him there with his son.

Nell did as she was told, hoped when she reached them that she hadn't called at an inconvenient time, and was warmly greeted. Luciano remembered their previous conversation and immediately said what a pity it was that Francesca's family had died out at Poggione.

'But not at Pratolino,' Nell was able to say, and then, seeing their interest, brought her grandmother's story up to date as briefly as she could.

'I know Marco, of course,' Father Pavese said, 'and Sergio Ruffini too, though he no longer attends Mass. But I didn't know of their connection with the Pizzoni family.' He thought about what Nell had told them, and picked out of it what now seemed most relevant to her.

'Your relatives' decision not to sell their farm – has that made a problem for you with your friends at the villa?'

'It's certainly been a headache for my husband,' Nell admitted ruefully. 'Now he must find another site, but nothing he's looked at so far is suitable.' Then a glimmer of amusement lit her face. 'I haven't pretended to like the idea of Sir Frank's hotel, but I haven't so far claimed any divine help in stopping it!'

The priest's rich chuckle made Luciano smile as well. 'I'm afraid the wheels of God grind more slowly than that as a rule.' Then he grew serious again. 'There's something your husband probably doesn't know about yet – a Franciscan monastery that has been closed down. With its inmates reduced to three old men, it couldn't continue as a working community.'

Nell asked the obvious question. 'It must have a church . . . therefore consecrated ground?'

'Of course; it has everything you would expect – a church, refectory, library, monks' cells – but also extensive grounds, because in happier days the monks were devoted agriculturalists. The buildings are old but sound – and beautiful. It was our fervent hope that they could be saved from being pulled down.'

'But time and weather, Father – don't they destroy old buildings that are left empty?'

'We hoped not to leave them empty,' he said sadly in answer to her question. 'Our dream was to convert them into a home and training school for deprived children, but it became clear that we could never afford what we wanted to do. The only option left to the Order was to find another buyer.' He understood the uncertainty in Nell's face. 'By all means tell your husband about it – there's no point now in not doing so. The place is called Carmanuolo: it's between here and Siena, and a caretaker remains on the premises.'

She thanked him, said goodbye, and remembered to collect Lucia's shopping from the housekeeper before setting off for the villa.

Even since she'd arrived less than two weeks ago, the growing heat had changed the landscape around her. On the hillsides the olive trees were in full leaf, and the winter-pruned vines were already garlanded with greenery. The road was still edged with wild flowers, but now they would have wilted by midday. It was a reminder of Tuscany's climatic extremes – bitterly cold in winter, hot as Hades in July and August.

But, walking along, her mind was more concerned with the deserted monastery she'd been told about. What had once been not only a sanctuary but also a hive of productive activity now stood empty for lack of young men willing to accept the discipline of monastic life. She couldn't help hoping that it would be of no interest to Giles, but having been given permission to tell him about it, that she must at least do.

Upset by the morning's drama in the kitchen, Lucia had for once failed to make their lunchtime pasta. But Frank Middleton looked pleased at the offer instead of wafer-thin slices of succulent prosciutto, to be eaten with wedges of Gianni's ripe, juicy melons. When this first course had been followed by veal, delicately flavoured with lemon and vermouth, his wife felt justified in teasing him about the '*cucina povera*'.

'We won't give you away to Sylvie,' she said with a smile, 'but at least admit that, thanks to Lucia's "peasant" cooking, we eat very well here.'

Still unsettled by the change in a woman who'd never before thought to poke gentle fun at him, he tried to sound in control of the conversation. 'There's a lot wrong with this country – the way it's governed for a start – but I'll agree the people make it easy to live here if you don't have to do business with them. Even that young hothead, Marco, would be likeable if he'd only learn a bit of common sense.'

Nell bit her tongue, then remembered her decision taken early on not to be steamrollered by Frank Middleton. She shook her head in reply to what he'd just said.

'I'm afraid that what you call sense, Sir Frank, Marco would call stupidity. As a young man you probably shared his stubbornness and went on to succeed; Marco believes he will, too.'

He glared at her across the table but took refuge in diversionary tactics, first banging his empty wine glass down. 'I'll tell you something else that's wrong with this place – it's run by women; it's matriarchal! Lucia's the boss in the kitchen; Sylvie henpecks her poor sod of a husband; and, between you and my wife, I can barely open my mouth for fear of being contradicted.'

'It's not what you're used to in Yorkshire?' Nell asked with a faint air of surprise.

'You're right, it's not. And the sooner we get back there the better, it seems to me.' Then he threw down his napkin as well and marched away into the house.

'Seriously displeased, would you say?' Nell asked after a moment. 'Or just reminding us not to push our luck too far?'

'*That*, I think,' Joan answered and even ventured a smile at her friend. 'I didn't realize it until we came here, but it's very good for him to be thwarted occasionally. What a lot I have to thank you for!'

'Not me; according to your husband, it's due to Italy's matri-archal air! And I think he suspects that the rot has set in – things won't be any different when he gets back to Huddersfield!'

On that happy note, they went their separate ways for the rest of the afternoon.

Nell was still alone when Giles returned, hot and disgruntled. She didn't even need to ask how his day had gone; frustration was written all over him.

'Promising place, maddening owners,' he said briefly. 'They're having second thoughts about selling – want to wait and see how they feel six months from now. No wonder Frank finds Italians irritating.'

Nell shook her head. 'He likes the people – he said so at lunch.' She was tempted to recount the rest of the conversation but decided against it. Time was when Giles would have found it funny, but she couldn't be sure of that now. 'It's just everything else that's wrong with Italy,' she finished up instead; 'everything but the nice, ordinary people.'

Giles now remembered why she'd wanted to stay behind that morning. 'Did you go to Pratolino and make your peace with Marco?'

'I didn't even get there,' she confessed and went on to describe the drama in the kitchen that had intervened. Having dealt with Carlotta's visit to the surgery, she finally mentioned her call at the *presbiterio*.

'I went just intending to enquire about old Luciano, but Father Pavese was there as well.' She repeated what the priest had told her, expecting Giles at least to be grateful for a new possibility, but he looked, if anything, more discouraged than before.

'Tomorrow's last hope is nowhere near Siena – and, really, Nell, a monastery! We probably wouldn't be able to touch a single stick or stone of the place without getting some ancient statute overturned, and that could take years in Italy.'

She'd been about to suggest that she would go with him to visit the monastery; instead, she merely hoped that Jonathan and Jacqueline would come back with something more positive to report.

'If they come back still on speaking terms, it will be a minor miracle,' Giles said wearily. 'I'm afraid your brother makes it quite clear to Jacqueline where his sympathies lie.'

'You can't be surprised about that,' Nell felt entitled to point out.

Giles left this unanswered but needed to find something else to say. 'Jonathan won't have had things all his own way; Jacqueline isn't Yorkshire born and bred for nothing. She reckons southern men not much of a challenge as a rule.'

Nell managed a smile. 'As dear Frank would say, happen she'll have had to change her mind today!' Then, disliking a wrangle that seemed futile, she spoke in a different tone of voice. 'I had the luxury of the pool to myself this afternoon; why don't you go and swim now, before the others get back?'

'Happen I will,' he agreed with a reluctant grin. 'What good ideas you have, Mrs Fanshawe.'

But he didn't have long to swim alone. Soon afterwards Jonathan tracked Nell down and reported that Jacqueline was already frolicking in the pool as well.

'How went the day?' Nell asked, quoting – very appropriately, Jonathan pointed out – from an enquiry about a much earlier battle.

'We bled on both sides,' he went on, smiling at his own quotation. 'That is, if you're asking about me and Jacqueline. As far as Giles is concerned, the day was wasted – the estate agent had omitted to mention a housing estate that couldn't *not* be noticed. Sad for the poor Contessa we interviewed needlessly.'

'But not your fault.'

'True, though still upsetting.' Not wanting to be asked what he and Jacqueline had fought about, he asked instead if Nell had been to see Marco. Once again she described how her own morning had been spent.

'Giles showed no interest in the monastery,' she finished up, 'and I'm not sorry. Beautiful old buildings soaked in centuries of prayer and praise shouldn't be bulldozed into rubble.'

'Why don't we go and see them before they are?' her brother suddenly suggested. 'At least, providing someone else can take us. You aren't to be trusted among Italian drivers who routinely enjoy discovering whose nerve will crack first – theirs or the man's next to them.'

'I'm not even volunteering,' Nell admitted, 'but if Beppe would like a day out, we could take Joan as well and go on and visit Siena.' Then she looked doubtful. 'Giles may want you to escort Jacqueline again tomorrow.'

'She'll insist on going with *him*. I'm afraid Miss Middleton is not impressed by the Ashley charms; one outing with me will have been enough.'

Nell stared at him with curiosity as well as affection in her face. 'Your charms are usually more than adequate. You mustn't feel obliged to try and alienate her on my behalf, and you can't really want to; even I can see that she's like one of those Wagnerian Rhine maidens – dangerously come-hitherish!'

'They're supposed to be heard, not seen,' he pointed out. 'There was a single moment today when Jacqueline seemed faintly likeable – she got angry because a frail, elderly woman had been need-lessly disappointed; apart from that, she played the part of the tiresome, spoiled minx admirably.'

'We've done well with the Middletons today, you and I,' Nell commented. 'You've probably offended *her*, and I've irritated her father. What perfect house guests we are, to be sure.'

Jonathan grinned but there'd been regret beneath what she'd said, and he thought it was time to move the conversation on. 'Have you given up trying to sell Frank the idea of helping Marco?'

'Well, I've given up hope of succeeding, but I'll keep on trying. Who knows? Like the drip of water on stone, I might wear him down.' Her smile faded into sudden sadness. 'I need *something* worthwhile to come out of our being here . . . to set against the grief of losing Giles.'

The desolation in her face made him grip her hands. 'Nell love, don't be so sure of that. He still needs *you*; I'd swear to it.'

'So would I, but it isn't enough,' she answered with the calmness of despair. 'He belongs in the Middleton camp now. What he's being offered is too seductive to be refused – it's not only Jacqueline; he can't resist being Frank's alter ego in London.'

Jonathan nodded, afraid that it was true. Then he risked a different question. 'Are you going to do anything about Bertrand? He can't look at you without giving himself away.'

'What is there to do?' Nell asked forlornly. 'I made my marriage vows to Giles, and Bertrand has a wife. Sylvie may only be that in name, but she's a working partner he wouldn't want to do without.' She smiled ruefully at her brother. 'To think we set out for a simple stay in Tuscany! It's lovely beyond words, and at least we know the truth about Francesca, but I shall be thankful to go home. Whatever she passed down to me, it wasn't an Italian relish for emotion piled on emotion. Please God, give me back a serene Anglo-Saxon life!'

Jonathan leaned over to kiss her cheek in a rare gesture of affection.

'There's no going back,' he said gently. 'We can only go on, and you know that as well as I do.'

# Sixteen

The outing to Carmanuolo looked threatened when Beppe had to admit what Nell realized she should have known: with Carlotta virtually one-handed for the time being, Lucia would need her husband there, not out driving with the *Inglesi*. But the conversation with Beppe was overheard, and soon afterwards Bertrand offered himself as chauffeur.

Nell looked doubtful. 'More important work not needing to be done? Sylvie not wanting to be looked after?'

Bertrand smiled at both questions. 'She is being collected by friends tomorrow, and there is nothing more I can do until I know if and where my masterpiece is to be built. *Enfin*, I'm entirely at your service.'

Nell reckoned she'd protested enough and produced her map of Tuscany without more ado. 'I've marked the place we want to visit – Carmanuolo – and then we thought perhaps lunch in Siena; we haven't been there yet.'

'And why not back via San Gimignano?' Bertrand suggested. 'It's a tourist trap now, I'm afraid, but still extraordinary, and beautifully placed on its hilltop.'

'We *are* tourists,' Nell pointed out. 'Let's do what tourists do!' Then she looked thoughtful. 'It's very fortuitous, your coming with us. Carmanuolo is a monastery now empty of monks that the Franciscans must dispose of – Father Pavese told me about it. Giles only sees it in terms of ancient buildings that Sir Frank wouldn't be allowed to destroy without a long legal battle. But *you* could see whether they're convertible.'

He smiled at the hope in her face and, omitting to say that it sounded very unlikely, agreed to do his best.

There was a marked lack of enthusiasm forthcoming from Giles the following morning when she explained that they would be out for the day.

'Why a remote, empty monastery, Nell? That isn't what tourists normally feel obliged to visit,' he pointed out irritably.

She omitted Bertrand's job of inspecting the buildings and merely said that Father Pavese had described them as beautiful and threatened – two good reasons for going to see them before it was too late.

Aware that his real objection couldn't be put into words, Giles merely commented that what she'd just said applied to most of Italy's cultural heritage.

'True, but unfortunately we can't go on and see it all,' she answered, leaving him with the feeling that she had just won – and he had lost – a small battle that might turn out to be important.

Frank Middleton was no more pleased than Giles had been when told that *his* wife would be out all day. 'I'd have thought Bertrand at least had something better to do with his time,' he said sourly.

'Apparently not,' Joan insisted. 'He offered to come with us.' Then she smiled at her husband. 'Sylvie will be out as well with friends – you'll have the villa to yourself; no one to irritate you at all!'

He tried to keep his end up by pointing out that it would make a pleasant change, but, by mid-morning, when Beppe brought coffee out to the terrace, he wasn't sorry to see Vittorio Guidi emerge from the kitchen quarters.

'We've missed you at the dinner table lately, Count,' he remarked almost genially.

'I was called away to a sick friend,' Vittorio explained, 'and came back to hear from Gianni about his sister's mishap. But she tells me her hand is mending now.'

Hesitantly, he risked a question that might irritate – or irritate if it *wasn't* asked. 'No news yet, Sir Frank, about another site? I suppose everyone else is out looking.'

'No news, and none likely, I reckon,' was the glum response. 'Giles and my daughter are certainly still looking; the others are just out enjoying themselves.'

Vittorio tactfully ignored this footnote. 'Gianni also mentioned that Sergio Ruffini had been unwell, so I called at Pratolino this morning. He is troubled by sciatica, poor man – a legacy of years of hard work, I'm afraid.'

'That's farming for you – much pain, little profit,' Middleton was glad to be able to point out.

'But a great deal of satisfaction, nevertheless! I was interested to see what Marco is doing there,' the Count went on gently. 'He's a very impressive young man.'

'Aye, and pig-headed too! Why can't he admit he's on to a loser?'

'With help, he wouldn't be,' Vittorio said, this time with unexpected firmness. 'I'm tempted to offer what help I can, but there's a problem.'

Never one to beat about the bush, Frank Middleton thought he knew what the problem was. 'My guess, Count, is that you're not a wealthy enough man to take a risk that might not pay off – probably won't, in fact.'

Vittorio merely smiled at the bluntness. 'That is probably true, but it's not the problem I had in mind. Marco still distrusts me because my name is Guidi. He would see my offer as an attempt to regain possession of the farm.'

'Pig-headed, like I said, and stuffed full of bloody silly notions about all for one and one for all – they haven't worked yet, nor will they.' But a rueful smile suddenly changed Middleton's face. 'I was going to add that he should learn a little sense, but I got properly put in my place for saying that to Nell Fanshawe! Come to think of it, she's done nothing but contradict me ever since she arrived.'

Taking this to be a criticism, Vittorio sounded rather stiff. 'In the words of your Prayer Book, she is "lovely and pleasant in all her ways". I think Giles Fanshawe is a very fortunate man.'

'I'm afraid I agree with you,' was the odd reply, before the subject of Giles's wife was waved aside. 'Happen I'll go and take a look at Marco's farm myself – might as well see what I wasn't allowed to buy. I don't usually get beaten by a whippersnapper.'

'But he and Nell are related, are they not? Perhaps you should have expected this defeat, Sir Frank!' Pleased with himself for having unusually scored a point, Vittorio smiled as he stood up and walked away to his own part of the house.

★   ★   ★

Mention of Father Pavese's name was enough to make the visitors welcome at Carmanuolo. The caretaker was bored, and people to talk to were a rare pleasure.

There was nothing lavish about the buildings he led them to – richness of ornamentation wouldn't have appealed to the Order's gentle founder, Nell remembered – but, in their simplicity and proper use of local wood and stone, they fitted into the Tuscan landscape as if they'd slowly grown there over the centuries. She saw Bertrand's quiet delight as he looked around, and felt all the more glad that he was with them.

The caretaker was proud of what he showed them, but his real regret was for the surrounding land, now idle and reverting to wildness – the monks, he said, had been such clever farmers. He seemed reluctant to see his unexpected visitors go, despite the largesse that Jonathan slipped into his hand when they said goodbye.

They drove away in silence until Joan said, 'How can such a place be destroyed. Surely *some* use could be made of it?'

'Father Pavese and his friends *had* a use for it,' Nell explained sadly. 'They wanted to make it a home and training school for deprived children – imagine them living there instead of in some drug-ridden Neapolitan slum.'

'So what went wrong? Lack of money, I suppose,' Bertrand answered his own question. 'Conversion would have been comparatively simple, but the likely running costs afterwards probably made it impossible. It's a tragic, wasted opportunity, though.'

Little more was said after that, and they were soon approaching Siena. With the car safely parked, they walked into the heart of the city: its famously beautiful Campo – a great fan-shaped space gloriously floored in russet, herringbone bricks. They walked, Nell rightly said, into the fourteenth century. Florence might belong to the Renaissance, but Siena was medieval.

With Jonathan plaintively calling attention to the time, they agreed to lunch first and settled at a *ristorante*'s outside table. With sustaining pizzas ordered and bread and wine in front of them, Bertrand confessed to having been there before.

'I made the mistake of coming in July, on the very day of the Palio! I can't describe the crowds, the noise, the interminable processions, and finally the race itself, round the outer rim of the Campo. It must be the most ferocious horse race in the world – nothing was barred except the jockeys actually killing each other. But the most frightening thing was the level of race fever; it infected even the most sensible-looking Sienese citizens to such an extent that I could have been watching a gladiatorial combat in the Colosseum in ancient Rome! I was thankful when it was over.'

'It's interesting,' Jonathan said thoughtfully. 'We reckon – rightly – that Italians are among the most civilized people on the planet, but even here there's still a latent streak of savagery beneath the surface. They hanged criminals upside down to die in public in fifteenth-century Venice – understandable then, you might say. But Mussolini and Claretta Petacci were treated in exactly the same way when they were caught and killed in Milan towards the end of the last war.'

The distress in Joan Middleton's face made Nell look a warning at her brother. 'No more horror stories, please . . . not today.'

He patted Joan's hand apologetically, and then savagery was put aside as the waiter brought their food.

Afterwards they strolled through the cavernous alleys leading off the sun-drenched Campo – a contrast of darkness and light echoed by the Cathedral's strangely striped facade of black and white marble.

San Gimignano, when they reached it, was less atmospheric. Nothing sinister was left now in its cluster of medieval towers. The little town drowsed in the afternoon heat with 'old unhappy, far-off things and battles long ago' forgotten; more useful now was it to relieve its throng of visitors of as much of their spending money as possible.

At last they returned to the car and headed back towards Poggione, this time with Nell sitting beside the driver, and Joan and Jonathan ready to nod off in the back seats.

'We've seen Italy in microcosm today,' Bertrand said. 'So much that's beautiful and so much that's drenched in the blood of a long and turbulent history.' He turned to smile at Nell. 'Is that a sententious enough statement for you?'

'Sententious,' she agreed, 'but true! Thank you for coming with us – it's been a memorable day.' She glanced round to see if the other two were asleep. 'Now it's time to think what happens next. If Giles has been on another wild-goose chase, I think it spells the end of Frank Middleton's Tuscan dream.'

'Which you won't mind at all,' Bertrand suggested.

'No, but I shall regret everyone else's disappointment. Couldn't your masterpiece be scaled down and make a gorgeous home for some rich man with taste enough to know what he is getting?'

'Easily, once I find the rich man,' Bertrand agreed with a smile.

'Sir Frank is wealthy enough,' Nell pointed out, 'but – taste apart – I'm afraid too many things about Italy irritate him! He'll go back to Huddersfield with a little sigh of relief.'

'What about you, Nell – is London calling, or have you discovered that you're more Italian than you thought?'

She hesitated for a moment, then answered honestly. 'I shall be glad to leave for reasons that have nothing to do with Tuscany, but part of me will belong here.' Not wanting to go on talking about herself, she asked him the same question, and he took longer to answer than she had done.

'We shall go back to Paris, Sylvie and I.' He stopped talking for a moment, then went slowly on. 'She could have left me all those years ago but chose not to, and I mustn't leave her now. Mostly thanks to her, we have a very successful, high-profile marriage and partnership – we're all the rage in Paris!'

'Nice for you,' Nell murmured, inadequately she felt. 'Everything you ever wanted, in fact.'

'Everything but this – that I shall miss *you* for the rest of my life.'

She was silenced for a moment, then whispered, 'I'm so sorry, Bertrand.'

'Don't be. I shall seem to be a fortunate man. No one else will know that in my heart I'll say "hello" to you every morning and "sleep well, my love" every night.' He turned to smile at her. 'You don't have to say anything at all!'

But, unsteadily, she answered at last. 'Am I at least allowed to say that I shall remember it as a gift you make me each day?'

'Yes, you can say that,' he agreed, and then they drove the rest of the way back in silence.

# Seventeen

They arrived back at the villa to find Frank Middleton in an odd mood – half-angry because they'd been away so long, but half-pleased as well. He had news he thought they wouldn't like, and began by looking at Bertrand.

'Your wife's gone to Venice for a day or two with her friends – apparently only the Venetians know how to make the fabrics she's interested in.' His tone of voice made it clear what he thought of this excuse. Then it was Nell's turn.

'Jacqueline telephoned; she and Giles can't get back tonight. It's nothing to worry about – they weren't hurt – but the car's having to be worked on. A Coca-Cola lorry braked too sharply in front of them and they went into the back of it. The mechanic will have it on the road again tomorrow.' He surveyed the four of them without enthusiasm. 'So it's just us at the dinner table, but at least the Count is back; that's something.'

Nell resisted the temptation to apologize for being only themselves and clearly not enough. There was an even stronger longing to ask who had been driving the car, except that she could guess the answer already; Miss Middleton was well known for leaving as little space as possible between herself and the vehicle in front.

'Where are they staying?' it seemed safe to ask instead, even though that question was pointless as well. If her husband's ambition to sleep with Jacqueline was about to be realized, it scarcely mattered whether they were somewhere in Tuscany or in Ultima Thule. But it seemed a savage irony that it should be *this* night, after her conversation with the man standing next to her that had touched her so deeply.

'They're in Cortona,' Middleton said. 'Nice town, Jacqueline reckoned, and they've found a comfortable hotel.' He smiled at Nell. 'No need for you to worry about Giles at all.'

She made herself smile back. 'Did she think to say whether it had been worth going – apart, of course, from discovering how nice Cortona is?'

He privately saluted an opponent worthy of his steel but managed to sound irritated. 'I didn't even ask. The important thing was to know they were both all right. Don't you agree?'

'We all do,' his wife said for her. Then she turned to smile at her companions. 'We've had a wonderful day, but now I think we're all in favour of a shower and a change of clothes before dinner.'

Gently but firmly she had taken charge and put an end to a duel between her husband and her friend that had gone on long enough. Even in the middle of her distress, Nell recognized the fact and found it comforting. Joan Middleton was her own woman at last. Thanks be to the Virgin Mary and all the saints in heaven who looked after lost and downtrodden women.

Dinner went smoothly, partly due to the Count's softening presence and partly to Lucia's inspired offering that even drew praise from Frank Middleton – pork tenderloin, with fennel steamed and then puréed, she happily explained, with rosemary, cream and *parmigiano*. Jonathan and Bertrand vied with each other to keep the conversation going, and there was no further mention of the *incidente stradale* that had kept two of the party in Cortona.

But alone at last in her bedroom, Nell knew it was time to decide what she must do next. Her immediate thought was to leave for London in the morning, before Giles could get back to the villa. Whatever grief went with her, it would be better than having to see a smiling Jacqueline announcing in everything but words that she had won. Certain that departure was the only thing left, Nell began to empty drawers of her clothes, but, as suddenly as she'd begun, she stopped again. Leaving would tell Giles, and the rest of them, that she'd prejudged him and found him guilty. It was tempting, but it wasn't fair. And, once gone, she wouldn't know what was going to happen next – was the hotel dream finally over, and the Tuscan adventure with it?

Almost unaware of a changed decision taken, she put her clothes away again and went to sit by the window instead. Scents and faint nocturnal noises drifted up to her from the garden, and she knew that what she'd said earlier to Bertrand was true. Even if she never came back again, what had been Francesca's home would in some way be her home too, and that thought brought something else to mind – she couldn't have left without saying goodbye to Sergio and Marco. Driven away from the window at last by the cool night air, she got into bed and – against all expectation – went to sleep.

It seemed important the next morning not to be seen waiting for the travellers to return. After Joan's morning lesson, Nell hid herself in her garden refuge and doggedly started to work. She was still there when Bertrand found her – sent by Joan to say that lunch was being brought out to the terrace. First, though, he put something in front of her on the table – an exquisite pen and ink sketch of the cluster of buildings they'd seen at Carmanuolo.

'A small keepsake,' he said. 'Drawn from memory and far from perfect, I'm afraid.'

'It's beautiful – that will more than do,' she answered simply.

'I've done something else as well,' Bertrand admitted. 'I've made a few suggestions for converting those buildings into a school. The priest you spoke of might think they're worth keeping in case some rich philanthropist should come riding by!'

'A "few suggestions" from the most noted architect in Paris given free of charge? Dear Bertrand, of course he'll treasure them.' She looked at him with a question in her face. 'Will you be very sad if the Middleton hotel is finally scuppered? Giles said that yesterday's prospect was the last one he had.'

'Disappointed, perhaps,' Bertrand answered. 'Professionally, that is. In another way, I think I shall be relieved. Marco's argument was very convincing – good land, rare in Italy, shouldn't be reserved for the use of a few wealthy visitors.' He smiled at her. 'It's been your argument all along – I'm glad I've caught up with you.'

She placed the sketch he'd given her carefully in her own folder of drawings and stood up. 'Time for lunch, you said; perhaps we'd better go.'

It was early evening, and Nell was in the courtyard helping Beppe water the pots around the pool when a car drove in. She didn't move, certain that the moment Giles and Jacqueline emerged from the car she would know that their relationship had changed. But Carlotta waved to her from the open door of the house – there was a telephone call for Signor Jonathan and he was nowhere to be found; she was needed to speak for him. When she was free again, there was only the empty car outside, and she was suddenly unable to go into the house and meet her husband again under Jacqueline's impertinent gaze.

She loitered in the garden, pretending to anyone who happened to notice her that she was dead-heading faded roses. But she couldn't hide indefinitely. When everyone else was likely to be assembled on the terrace, she put Beppe's secateurs away and climbed up towards the house.

Sheathed this evening in flame-coloured silk, Jacqueline was devoting herself to the Count. Giles, looking tired and withdrawn, listened while Bertrand and Joan tried to interest him in their visit to the monastery. It left Jonathan with his host – two men without a single thought in common. Watching them for a moment unseen, Nell had the impression of actors 'frozen' on stage before the curtain went up. She stepped into view, tension was released, and the action began – this was the moment they'd been waiting for.

She stopped in front of Giles and kissed his cheek. 'Nice to have you back safe and sound.'

He was able to smile at her. 'Nice to be here, Mrs Fanshawe. I'm glad you had a good day yesterday – I've been hearing about it.'

'You were right not to be interested in Carmanuolo,' Nell suggested. 'We all agreed that such a lovely place *mustn't* be knocked down.'

Frank Middleton suddenly intervened. 'What was Giles not to be interested in knocking down?'

Nell turned to face him. 'Only a Franciscan monastery that has been closed for lack of novitiates; the three elderly men left weren't enough to keep it going. Father Pavese and his friends hoped to convert it into a haven for neglected slum children – a home and training school combined. But the government refused to finance it and private philanthropists are hard to come by now as well.'

She lifted her hands in a little gesture that brushed the missing monks and the deprived children aside, and accepted the sparkling white wine that Beppe had just poured for her. There was a moment's awkward silence while they each considered who should say something next, and then Lucia appeared with the evening's antipasto – roasted peppers stuffed with slivers of pancetta and garlic-scented breadcrumbs.

Seated where she was, Nell could see Giles across the table, with Jacqueline sandwiched between him and the Count. They were intensely aware of each other; nothing unexpected about that, of course, but something – presumably a sense of guilt, she thought – was making Giles, at least, look strained and disinclined to join in the conversation. Jacqueline, on the other hand, was talkative enough for both of them and very funny on the subject of their brush with the strong arm of the Italian traffic police.

'They finally agreed not to charge us with any wrongdoing,' she ended up carelessly. 'It might have had something to do with Giles's bribe, but my eyelashes were just as useful, I reckon!'

Giles joined in the laughter against himself, but seemed anxious to talk of something other than themselves. He congratulated Vittorio Guidi on the standard of service available in even a small Italian town, and then seemed to challenge Middleton at the end of the table. 'It would have taken days, if not weeks, at home to get the car repaired; here the mechanic seemed happy to work late into the night.'

'All right,' came the grudging reply. 'I grant you some things are better here.' Nell waited for him to add, as Beppe came to remove their plates, that Italians made more cheerful waiters too, but perhaps he realized in time that Beppe's grasp of English had improved enough for him to understand.

She found the evening a trial, not so much for itself but for the moment when it would end and she and Giles had to face each other. There was no doubt in her mind that, in one way or another, the relationship between him and Jacqueline had changed, but his attitude defeated her; she couldn't guess what had happened or what would come next.

She made the excuse of a slight headache to escape from the *salone* early. She got ready for bed, then sat down as usual by the window, telling herself that a local nightingale might redeem a miserable night by singing for her. She was still there, waiting, when Giles came into the room, and his drawn face made her speak without effort or thought after all.

'You look so tired and unhappy. Just tell me what it is you

want – I promise I won't make a scene, or weep, or throw myself out of the window. I've had time enough to get used to the idea that we no longer have a marriage.'

'More than time enough,' he agreed slowly, 'but the idea is yours, not mine. It never was, even when I was doing my damnedest to wreck it.' He came to share the window seat with her. 'May I tell you what happened yesterday, or are you so sick of the subject that you can't bear to listen?'

'I'll listen – but ask a question first. Was Jacqueline driving the car?'

'Yes, she always wants to, and she normally drives fast but well; yesterday it was fast but dangerously because she was in a bad mood – tired of what we were doing, wanting a more exciting time than life at the villa, even irked by seeing the rest of you drive away on an outing she wasn't included in. She only hit the lorry because she was tailgating it, to get the driver to move over. I think the police realized it, but, as she said, the eyelashes helped to get us off.'

'She could have killed you both,' Nell murmured almost to herself. Then she took a breath and spoke more firmly. 'Now the scene moves to the "nice town of Cortona and its comfortable hotel", I take it?'

'Yes – it was late by then and we'd had nothing to eat. Afterwards I just wanted to crawl into bed; even if it was on offer, a night of unbridled passion was beyond me after the day we'd had. But Jacqueline clearly expected me to ask for it; I wasn't playing the game properly. She began to talk about you – "poor Nell – what she must be imagining?" and much more of the same. To end the conversation, I asked if she would pretend to you that we'd spent the night together. She smiled at me and said there'd be no need; she'd insist the opposite, and the more she insisted, the more you would believe that she was lying.'

'She was probably right,' Nell felt obliged to agree. 'Vicious but right. What happened next?'

'I walked away to my room. Beautiful as she is, and possessed of some magnetism that she uses on men, I couldn't have touched her then if she'd been Helen of Troy and the Venus de Milo rolled into one. I just felt degraded in some way, and old and tired as well.'

There was silence in the room until Nell found something to

say. 'She won't accept defeat without trying to hurt you – through her father presumably.'

'She might, but he's the only human being she loves, and she knows that I serve him well. I told you once before that sooner or later she'd leave me behind – it will be sooner, that's all; now, in fact.'

Nell asked a different question. 'What else happened yesterday – did you find anything?'

'We found what might do very well, but the estate has been the subject of a long-running legal battle within the family. The people we saw say it's coming to an end and they're confident they'll win, but we can't proceed until the judge gives his ruling.'

'Meanwhile, everyone stays here?' She saw him nod, and then went on herself. 'Giles, I don't think I can bear to. Even if I'm wrong about Jacqueline and her father's intention to get you into their family, I'd still rather leave. Forgetting her for a moment, I can't like Frank Middleton and I think he has an equal dislike of me, so it seems wrong to be here as his guest.'

'Is there more to it than that, Nell?' Giles asked quietly. 'God knows I wouldn't blame you if you can't bear to be here with me, either.' He watched her for a moment, fearful that he knew a reason for the sadness in her face. 'Does Bertrand have anything to do with your wanting to leave? I know that it's you he loves, not his wife.'

Nell shook her head. 'He won't, nevertheless, abandon Sylvie, any more than Joan would abandon her husband if Vittorio should ask her to. They're constant people who keep the vows they take. My own vows still hold too, but I think you need time to decide about yours.'

Giles took hold of her hands and gripped them hard. 'I need time, but I need you as well. Please stay, Nell, unless it's just too much to ask.'

A faint, rueful smile lifted some of the strain from her mouth. 'If I agree, it may only be because Jacqueline will hate it so much – I'm afraid it's an unworthy reason for staying!'

'I can give you a better one,' Giles said unexpectedly. 'Frank wants to see Pratolino and he hopes you'll go with him.'

Silenced by surprise for a moment, she finally managed to ask, 'How did that come about?'

'The Count told him that *he'd* been and had come away so impressed that he wanted to help Marco himself. He can ill afford it, of course, but his main worry was that Marco would refuse help coming from a Guidi. Frank won't go out of idle curiosity – there's always a purpose in anything he does.'

Nell considered her next question. 'Do we warn Marco or not?'

'I think so – he mustn't let his political hackles rise this time. Can you persuade him to be tactful?'

'Sergio must do the persuading, I think; Marco will listen to his grandfather. Your own job will be even harder – to persuade Frank to behave like any other appreciative visitor, instead of a domineering tycoon seeing what he can interfere in next.'

For once Giles let the criticism go unchallenged, aware that there was truth in it. 'I'll do my best,' he said instead. Then he gently touched her face. 'Dear Nell, please go to bed; you look all in. But thank you for everything, far more than I can say.'

# Eighteen

Out early the next morning, Nell was scarcely aware for once of what normally gave her so much pleasure – the moment when the sun climbed above the hills across the valley, washed the landscape free of mist and bathed it in golden light instead. Today it rose unnoticed; there was too much to think about.

She'd told Giles she would stay despite Jacqueline's hostility; but what if Frank Middleton made it clear that she'd outstayed her welcome? She knew she hadn't been wrong about his plans for the future, and his daughter would see to it that he understood how seriously the plans had gone awry.

That thought brought with it another anxiety – his sudden interest in Pratolino. A generous wish to help was hard to believe in; surely it was more likely that he meant to outmanoeuvre the Ruffinis if he could? Imagination now running riot, she was pulled up short by an unexpected sound – the flat Yorkshire vowels of the man himself behind her.

'You're an early riser too, I see. But it's usually thinking time for me; I don't reckon much to what I'm told is called communing with nature.'

Recovering from the shock of finding him there, Nell said what first came into her head. 'I suspect you don't reckon much to nature at all, Sir Frank, and it makes me wonder why you suddenly want to go to Pratolino.'

To her intense surprise, a smile touched his face for a moment. 'You've put a spoke in my wheel, Nell Fanshawe, but I'll say this for you: you're the most honest woman I've ever met. I think you guessed what I wanted to happen all along – am I right?'

'It was scarcely a guess,' she pointed out since he seemed to count honesty a virtue. 'You wanted Giles as your son-in-law as well as your right-hand man, and your daughter wanted him as *her* husband, not mine? Am *I* right?'

'It's about the size of it,' he agreed, 'but you could say as well that they took a real shine to each other; that's what put the idea into my head.'

'Jacqueline is very alluring,' Nell felt obliged to concede. 'You must have been fairly sure you'd win.'

'I was, but – since we're being honest – I underrated you. You haven't been here long but, apart from getting in my way, you've made a new woman of my wife and a different man of Bertrand. I scented trouble that first day I met you at the airport. I should have sent you straight back to London there and then.'

Nell thought he sounded more irritated with himself now than with her, but her next question might upset him again. 'Am I allowed to know what Giles's new future is to be – plan B, as it were?'

Middleton looked surprised. 'I want him in charge in London, of course. I'm told I must slow down, and I'm counting on him. He hasn't made up his mind yet, that's all. You don't reckon much to me, I know, but I hope you won't make it difficult for him to accept the job.'

'Giles will make the decision himself.' Nell said simply. 'Now, can we talk about Pratolino? Before I take you there, I'd like to be sure the Ruffinis won't regret your visit. You insisted to Marco that farming is a lost cause here – so what interest can it have for you?'

'I don't know yet whether it has any at all, but I'm going to find out. The Count's a clever man for all his poetry nonsense and he's convinced that Marco deserves help. If he's right, I'm better placed to provide it than he is. Now will you go with me, or not? I could go alone, but young Marco isn't inclined to trust me.'

'I'll go with you,' she said slowly, 'but I shall tell Sergio as well to remember he's a Tuscan, with a keen eye for anything that has to do with money.'

Middleton nodded approvingly, apparently bearing her no ill-will for what he might have regarded as an insult.

Then she thought of one more thing to say. 'Will the Count mind you stepping in, if he wanted to help himself?'

'Not if he's the sensible man I take him for – he can't afford it, and he realizes that Marco might reject anything that comes from a Guidi.'

'Yes, it's probably true,' Nell agreed thoughtfully. She looked at Middleton with sudden appeal in her face. 'Will you remember that Marco might not be an easy young man for anyone to help?'

'I'll take it as certain that he won't be,' Middleton replied. 'I don't mind that – it's a scrounger I can't abide.'

Liking him for the first time, Nell smiled. 'If you've had enough of nature for one morning, shall we go in to breakfast?'

Before she could make her call to Pratolino, a telephone conversation with his colleagues at La Scala resulted in Jonathan announcing that he must make a return visit to Milan. The scenery that was being built there would be shipped to London, but only he could be sure that it would work on Covent Garden's different stage. He'd promised to catch an afternoon train and stay at least one night in the city.

To have Jacqueline follow him away from the breakfast table was the last thing he expected, and he was left speechless for a moment when she asked to go with him to Milan.

'You're joking,' he said hopefully at last. 'You think opera is for sissies, and you don't have a very high opinion of me.'

'Both true,' she agreed, 'but I'd like to come all the same. I can do some serious shopping in Milan, and I need a break from the Villa Guidi right now.'

She spoke in her usual offhand way, but something about her wasn't quite as usual. He fought against feeling sorry for her – the very idea was ridiculous – but at the moment she seemed as nearly forlorn as the rich man's spoiled brat could get. The contretemps with the car hadn't ended as it should have done, and probably for the first time in her life she was having to work out why not. If – as seemed likely – Giles had now slipped out of her net, she might reasonably want to get away – from him and perhaps even more from Nell.

'Let's get things clear,' he said at last. 'I'm going to Milan to work, not to give you a more exciting time than you're having here. I'll escort you there, find you a hotel room and even bring you back, but that's the extent of the Ashley guided tour. English is widely spoken there; you'll have no difficulty buying anything you want. Oh, and one more thing – make sure your father knows this is your idea, not mine.'

'I've had more enthusiastic escorts,' Jacqueline pointed out. 'If I weren't so desperate, I'd tell you to keep your guided tour.'

'On that promising note, let us part company. Beppe and I will be leaving for Florence to catch the train at two, with you if you're ready, without you if you're not.'

Then he went looking for Nell and found her finishing a telephone call to Sergio Ruffini.

'You look a mite anxious,' he said. 'Anything wrong?'

She shook her head. 'I hope not, but F.M., prodded into it by the Count, wants me to take him to Pratolino. I've just been warning Sergio and asking him to keep Marco at least civil to the great man.'

Jonathan thought for a moment. 'It's quite a volte-face, isn't it? Is he just going to throw a bit more of his considerable weight around, or do we see a glimmer of business interest? After all, he's now stuck with two small farms that he probably doesn't know what to do with.'

'There's that, of course,' Nell agreed, 'but to give the devil his due, I suspect him of actually wanting to help Marco, if he finds what he's looking for – evidence of sound management and real hope for the future.'

'Well, he'll find that all right, but railing against bloated plutocrats and the evils of capitalism won't help Marco's cause.'

'I know – that's why I spoke to Sergio first. We're to go over later this morning.' Then she remembered something else. 'Why were you looking for me?'

'Only to tell you what my own Middleton chore is: I'm to take Jacqueline to Milan – she's sick of the Villa Guidi.'

'You could have refused,' Nell commented, 'but perhaps you wanted to be helpful.'

'Something like that. By being really churlish I nearly got her to change her mind, but I think an extravagant shopping spree is to make up for what she seems to have lost. She hasn't had that happen before and it's smarting a bit.'

'Not too churlish in that case,' Nell suggested. 'You can't sit and glower at each other all the way to Milan.'

'Jacqueline can glower if she wants to – I shall be re-reading *War and Peace*,' he explained. 'I do it every three years and it gets better each time – that's genius for you.'

Nell agreed that it was, and decided that any more advice on how to treat his travelling companion would be fruitless; Jonathan would deal with her in his own way.

Her personal ordeal, approaching more quickly, was really what needed to be thought about. There'd been no time since break-fast to talk alone to Giles, but when he emerged from his usual morning session in the office, she asked if he was coming to Pratolino with them.

'No, it's to be a friendly visit, not a deputation. Frank's happy to walk down to the farm, but I'll have the car waiting to bring you back – it would be a climb for him in the midday heat.' He smiled at her anxious face. 'Cheer up, my dear – if he proposes something the Ruffinis don't like, they can always turn it down.'

'So they can,' she agreed and then put another worry into words. 'How is he with you now?'

'The same as he always is. He's not a petty man, Nell. If some-thing doesn't come off, that's the end of it. If we don't get the Cortona estate in the next week or two, the hotel dream will be written off, too – there are always new opportunities. I suppose that's why I like working for him so much.'

She remembered what Joan had said of her husband: he fought hard but fairly; perhaps that was what she in turn should have told Sergio.

Half an hour later Middleton emerged, ready for another encounter with nature, dressed informally in pale linen suit and panama hat; clearly, as Giles had said, theirs was to be a friendly visit. On the brief walk down the track, she was asked to explain her exact relationship to the Ruffinis.

Nell thought for a moment. 'Sergio's mother was my great-grandfather's sister, so it's a distant connection, but even those matter to Italians,' she explained. '*La famiglia* is still important here, even in these modern days.'

'You don't take much to modern days, I seem to think,' Middleton suggested.

Nell's slow smile appeared. 'The Count did once accuse me of wanting time to run backwards, and it's true that I regret the passing of what seems to have been a kinder, less merciless world than the present one.'

'Sentimental, that's what you are,' she was told, but it was mildly said. 'I expect you still weep when you hear "Land of Hope and Glory" played.'

'Most of Elgar's music makes me weep,' she admitted and saw him look pleased to have won a point.

But they were approaching the archway to the farmyard now, and small talk was put aside; he'd come for a good look round, and there was plenty to see, even here – outbuildings properly maintained, machinery not new but kept bright and clean . . . everything that spoke of good husbandry and management. Sergio was waiting for them, and then an unsmiling Marco appeared, driving a small tractor. On this, he said, *il Signore* could be taken to several vantage points, to see the work going on.

When they'd set off, Nell, left with Sergio, held up her hands with fingers crossed, but he shook his head.

'I think it will be all right. Signor Middleton need only be interested – and, if not, why has he come? – and Marco will respond.' Seeing that she still looked doubtful, he went on. 'If they come back too quickly, we shall know that I am wrong.'

But what was "too quickly" – ten minutes or thirty? Nell didn't know, but when there was still no sign of them half an hour later, she was ready to believe that Marco had overturned the tractor on one of the steep vineyard slopes and the visit had ended in disaster. But just as Sergio was setting out glasses on the terrace table, tractor, driver and passenger reappeared, with no damage visible. Nothing else was visible either: no smiling faces, no air of pleasure shared; they might, she thought, have been strangers sharing a rather uncomfortable taxi ride.

But it was now Sergio's turn to play host, and it was a role he enjoyed. He offered his guests the delicious white wine Nell had sampled on an earlier visit with Jonathan, so she knew what to expect. One sip was followed by another one swallowed more slowly before Middleton gave his verdict, with a faint air of surprise.

'It's good . . . it's very good,' he suggested.

Marco's set face almost smiled. 'It's good, but we can make it even better with another grape added to the mix; but that is for next *vendemmia*-time.'

While the wine was drunk, the conversation was general, about Tuscany and its rural population. Many people had left, Marco admitted, but their new surroundings made few of them happy. City life, even with all its conveniences, didn't suit men and women who had country ways in their blood.

Frank Middleton seemed disinclined to talk, and Nell waited for the moment when he decided he'd been affable long enough. He'd leave and the visit would have done nothing but waste Marco's precious time.

Then, as if he'd been waiting to drive them into asking what his intentions were, he pushed his glass away and placed both hands on the table.

Speaking to Sergio and Marco, he suddenly said, 'Listen, please. You've got skill, energy and a sound basis for something good here. What you haven't got is enough workable land – most of it's down in the valley which I now own.'

Sergio looked across at his grandson, then answered reluctantly. 'We should ask to buy it from you but we can't – it would take all our working capital; we should have nothing to invest.'

'I realize that,' Middleton said, 'so here's my proposition – take it or leave it as it stands, no bargaining. I give you the two farms I own—' He broke off and turned to Nell. 'Better translate this for me; I don't want any misunderstanding. I make the Ruffinis an outright gift of my land. In return, they make me a gift each year of a case of the wine we've just drunk and a case of their best, cold-pressed olive oil.'

Nell duly translated what she'd heard, suddenly doubted it, and stared at him in astonishment. He simply nodded; he'd stated his terms, there was nothing more to be said. Then, terrified that Marco might feel obliged to reject a gift offered from across the political divide he set such store by, she wanted to cry out to Sergio, 'Don't let him refuse . . . speak for him if necessary.'

But Sergio was looking at his grandson, waiting for the small nod of agreement that he needed. When it came, he rose to his feet, as did Marco then, and Middleton too. Smaller than the other two men, he was still a dignified figure as he held out his hand. 'We accept a very generous gift, Sir Frank, but wish to change the terms a little – you will receive red wine too, the best we can make; we aim to overtake Brunello before long!'

With a handshake exchanged, emotion got the better of Sergio, and, for the first time in his life, Frank Middleton was embraced by another man. Then it was Nell's turn to be kissed and hugged as well. Marco didn't go that far, but his dark eyes shone with excitement. She thought it was doubtful that he could wait for them to leave before he went out to examine what would soon be theirs. He'd want to walk over it, feel the ground beneath his feet, before he really believed what was happening.

More wine was poured and the future toasted, and Middleton explained that Nell's husband would see to the legal change of ownership; then he got ready to leave.

But suddenly Marco spoke. 'The olive harvest isn't until December – you wouldn't want to come then; but why not all of you come back for *vendemmia* in early October? It's the high moment of our year.'

'We just might,' Middleton surprisingly agreed. 'My daughter will probably insist on it.' Then goodbyes were said, and he and Nell set off back through the archway.

'Thank you,' she said simply when they were out of earshot. 'I can't find any more words than that.'

'They'll do,' he grunted. 'Now let's find Giles. I'm too old to pretend I'm a mountain goat climbing up that track you led me down. I need a comfortable ride back to the villa before I face one of Lucia's fifty-seven varieties of pasta.'

# Nineteen

When they got back, Nell found her brother eating the early lunch that had thoughtfully been provided for him. A small holdall beside him suggested that he was ready to leave for Milan, and Nell pointed to it with a smile.

'If I didn't know you for a kind-hearted man, I might suspect you of planning to lope off, leaving Jacqueline behind.'

'She's even now getting ready, I'm afraid – no chance.' He observed his sister for a moment. 'That was a diversion; I can see you're big with news. How did the visit go?'

'Almost unbelievably!' She explained what had happened and saw a mixture of astonishment and pleasure in his face. 'If Jacqueline doesn't know about it, perhaps you shouldn't be the one to tell her,' she finished up. 'Let's leave it to Frank himself.'

'Who'd have thought it?' Jonathan marvelled. 'Beneath that forbidding exterior beats a generous heart after all. Let it be a lesson to us not to think we know what's going to happen next!'

Then he spoke instead about himself. 'I'll make sure Jacqueline gets back here, Nell, but after that I must be on my way back to London. There's work piling up, and I'm sick of this lump of plaster on my arm – they said a month, so it ought to be able to come off soon. What about you here – will you be all right?'

She gave his hand a little pat. 'I agreed to stay – promised Giles we'd work out our future at home, not here. He thinks the Cortona prospect will go through, in which case I suppose we'll be here for several more weeks. If it doesn't, we'll be following you back quite quickly.'

'What will you remember most about Tuscany – the place, I mean, not what's happened here?'

'Its colours, I think,' she answered after a moment or two. 'Grey stone, russet tiles, every shade of green, and an ineffably blue sky. I know there are incomparable cities here, but it's the landscape that matters to me most. Whatever happens, I shan't regret coming.'

'Nor I,' Jonathan agreed, smiling at her. 'Francesca would be pleased.'

Then, as Beppe appeared to collect his holdall, he leaned over to kiss her cheek. '*Ciao, cara, arrivederci presto.* Pray for me that Jacqueline's changed her mind about coming.'

But she was waiting in the courtyard by the car, looking pointedly at her watch.

'I can't believe it,' he said cheerfully. 'A more than punctual female! Nell is never actually late, but there's always a nail-biting moment when you think she's going to be.'

He offered her the front seat, which she took without a word, thereby ensuring that Beppe would spend the journey into Florence hurling remarks over his shoulder at the passenger in the back seat.

At the station he asked if she would like something to read; no, she said – reading in trains made her feel sick. He suggested a snooze instead and, once they were settled in a compartment, pulled out his dog-eared copy of Tolstoy's masterpiece, at which she simply lifted an eyebrow. His advice was ignored; instead of sleeping, she stared out of the window but, when he glanced at her from time to time, he found himself again almost feeling sorry for her. However mixed her motives had been in trying to wreck Nell's marriage, one of them might have been a painfully real infatuation. Giles was an attractive, clever man, likely to have stood out among her provincial admirers, and there was always an extra charm attached to a prize that seemed to be out of reach.

Thinking this, he looked across at her again and now found her staring at him.

'Are you always as boring as this?' she wanted to know. 'Or am I being stood in the corner till teacher says I can go back to the rest of the class?'

The pert question made him suddenly angry with her. 'Admit that the accident in Cortona was your fault and you can rejoin the rest of us any time you like.'

It brought her bolt upright to face him across the table. 'The fool of a lorry driver braked too sharply to avoid a chicken or something equally stupid. The policeman didn't charge *me*.'

'No, because the poor devil had accepted the bribe Giles knew he wouldn't refuse.'

She glowered at him – he made a note to tell Nell that – and finally decided what to say. 'I *might* have been driving a little bit too close – will that do?'

'It's a start,' Jonathan agreed.

There was silence for a moment while she thought what to say next. 'I suppose you'll go off carousing with your friends tonight.' It left unsaid what she could do, alone in a strange city whose language she didn't speak.

The question had been exercising him for some time; he'd even been waiting for her to point out that he'd been her father's uninvited guest for several days. Ordinary decency seemed to insist that he must now pay his dues, especially since she hadn't reminded him of the Middleton hospitality he'd received.

'I'll be dining with friends,' he admitted. 'When we get to the hotel, I'll ring and ask to bring you along if you like. They do speak English, but they're more likely to forget and overwhelm you with a flood of Italian.'

'I'd rather drown than die of boredom – I'll risk it,' she replied, and soon afterwards they were travelling through the outskirts of Milan.

At its grandiose station – a true monument to the Fascist era – the survival of the fittest was the general rule in the fight to secure a taxi. But either Jonathan's arm in a sling or Jacqueline's short skirt stood them in good stead. They were even helped aboard by a brace of young men and sped on their way to the Hotel Manin.

'It's not your usual five-star hostelry,' Jonathan warned her, 'but it's comfortable and friendly.'

'Old-fashioned, I suppose you mean,' she guessed with deadly accuracy, but the grin that marked the point she'd scored was free of malice for once, and he didn't argue with what she'd said.

After his telephone call at the hotel, she *was* included in the evening's supper party. Even in a country with an unfair quota of beautiful young women, he admitted to himself that she didn't do badly for England's sisterhood; in fact, his male friends were considerably impressed and appeared not to mind that her Italian conversation was limited to *si*, *non* and *grazie*.

At the end of the evening, back at the Manin, he explained that she would have to spend the following evening on her own.

'Perhaps you can be busy gloating over the day's purchases,' he suggested hopefully.

'Let me guess how *your* evening will be spent – with the gorgeous Giovanna we met tonight?' she asked.

Jonathan shook his head. 'Much more exotic – the girl in question will be Japanese, the tragic heroine of what is Puccini's masterpiece.'

Opera again – Jacqueline had lost interest. 'Why not risk spending time with a real female? More fun, I should have thought.'

'Butterfly is real enough for me, especially tomorrow night. The scheduled diva is sick and a young soprano I know at Covent Garden has been sent for in a hurry. She'll be making her house debut, and La Scala audiences are about the most critical there are.'

Jacqueline watched him with a faint smile. 'You can wave a little Union Jack to let her know you're there.'

He looked down his fine straight nose. 'This is La Scala, Milan, not the vulgar last night at the Proms. Now, tomorrow I shall be working all day. If you get worn out with shopping, there's free seating in the Cathedral, and da Vinci's *The Last Supper* in the refectory of Santa Maria delle Grazie is generally thought to be worth a visit. My plan is to go back to Poggione the following morning. Will you have bought enough clothes by then?'

'For the time being,' she agreed and went off to her room.

He didn't see her the next morning before he left the hotel and realized that it was a relief not to; being with her felt like being engaged in a challenging but tiring duel, and he preferred to choose companions who would be less hard work.

Immersed in the backstage world of the opera house with his Italian colleagues, he forgot about her. Only as the time came that evening to take one of the seats reserved for special visitors did he remember her with a faint twinge of regret; the poor misguided girl should be here watching something she'd never forget.

The atmosphere in the house was electric – a new, unknown singer to be judged, and probably found wanting; foreign too – that added extra spice. Jonathan sent up a little prayer for his compatriot and then watched the curtain rise. She began, understandably, with a slight tremor of nervousness in her voice; but it was a beautiful voice, and he could feel the audience settling down to listen attentively.

By the time they'd reached the exquisite love-duet that ended the first act, he knew there would be no need of supporting flags – even the hard-bitten Milanese beside him was in tears. A new star in the operatic galaxy had just been born.

He made no attempt to seek her out after the performance – she would be surrounded by people; better to tell her in London how wonderful her debut had been. When the wild applause finally began to die down, he edged his way through the crowd in the foyer and, unexpectedly, glimpsed someone else he knew – Jacqueline Middleton, looking lost and lonely. When he managed to reach her, she smiled shakily at him, a different girl from the confident, careless, would-be worldling he was used to.

'I thought I'd give opera a try,' she said, hoping to sound her normal self. 'You might have told me it was going to be like that – a bit shattering.'

'I thought I did; you just weren't listening then. Now, let's get out of this crowd; no need for a taxi – we're within walking distance of the hotel.' He piloted her through the crush towards the door and then out into the street.

They walked in silence for a little while, but at last Jacqueline spoke. 'She did well, didn't she – your friend? The audience certainly thought so.'

'More than well; if angels sing in heaven, and I feel sure they do, they must sound as Amanda sounded tonight.'

Jacqueline was beginning to recover now. 'Speaking of angels, I've noticed that you go to church with your sister. I thought Catholics were the old women dressed in black who never stop curtsying in front of statues of the Virgin Mary – I didn't know men were involved as well.'

'The Pope is usually a man,' Jonathan ventured to point out.

Silenced for a moment, a little further on she spoke again. 'It's a very irritating habit of yours – always having the last word. I warn you, your wife will hate it if and when you have one.'

'I'll try to remember,' he promised, and then the hotel was in sight and the extraordinary evening at an end.

*   *   *

The train journey back to Florence the following morning was no more talkative than the outward one had been until Jonathan suddenly fired a question at his companion.

'What made your father want to build a hotel in Tuscany – a different sort of business venture from ball bearing factories and long-distance haulage, and shipbuilding in Greece?'

He expected her to shrug the question off, but instead she gave him a serious answer. 'You might find it hard to believe that he wanted to create something beautiful as well as useful. He'd seen some of Bertrand's work in Paris and reckoned he'd found the man he needed.'

'Disappointing for both of them if it doesn't come off,' Jonathan said; 'even though I still think Marco was right to hold on to his farm.'

'Well, Pratolino's safe – better than safe; the Ruffinis are being given the other two farms my father owns. He told me about it just before we left. I'll kill them if they let him down and sell the extra land off to some other developer as soon as he goes back to England.'

'So young and yet so cynical,' Jonathan commented. 'I suppose you warned him of the risk?'

'Hardly, with your sister there as well. I'd no mind to risk being torn limb from limb.'

Jonathan grinned but answered very firmly. 'They won't let him down and he knows it. *You* could trust people a little more. Why don't you?'

'Because I see too many of them trying to oil their way into his confidence. That's what I liked about Giles – he just wants to help my father, not get something out of him.' There was a note of genuine sadness in her voice that made him speak gently.

'I think he'll go on wanting to help. Nell won't stand in the way of his doing that.'

Jacqueline stared at him with a mixture of regret and irritated puzzlement in her face. 'Why couldn't she settle for Bertrand and let me have Giles?' She anticipated what might be coming and hurried on. 'I know, you don't have to tell me again – marriage vows! I suppose even my father must have some old-fashioned notion about observing them, or he'd have parted company with my stepmother years ago.'

He moved suddenly to grab her hands resting on the table. 'Listen to me carefully. Last night when we came out of the opera house, there were tear stains on your face – proof, I thought, that Jacqueline Middleton wasn't beyond hope of becoming a sensitive, interesting human being after all; she was beginning to understand something about love and life and death, and how all of it could be made bearable by overwhelming beauty. It seems I was wrong – you're still in the corner the class as far as I'm concerned until you care to admit that you and your father have in Joan Middleton someone neither of you deserves.'

There was a long pause before she found something to say. 'I think you're the rudest, most objectionable man I've ever met.'

'Good; otherwise I might think there was something seriously wrong with me.'

Another pause. 'I did warn you about always having the last word,' she finally muttered.

'So you did.' Then, to her surprise, he smiled at her. 'I'll let you have it this time.' He picked up his book, and nothing more had been said when the train deposited them at Florence station, and Giles's fair head could be seen above the people milling around the platform barrier.

# Twenty

Giles quickly explained to Jacqueline why he was there instead of Beppe – Joan Middleton had wanted him to be the one to tell her that her father had been unwell in the night. But he shook his head at the sudden fear in her face.

'My dear, he's quite all right now. We were worried at the time, but the doctor's certain that it wasn't a heart attack – only a severe indigestion pain after a heavy meal and a tiring and even hotter day than usual. He needs to rest more, that's all.'

'Then he needs me to see that he does. I'll drive, Giles – I want to get back quickly,' Jacqueline insisted.

'No, I'll drive, as fast as I safely can,' he corrected her gently. 'You don't have to agonize all the way back to the villa – he's being very well looked after.'

She hovered on the edge of saying that her stepmother wouldn't be of use, but Jonathan's warning eye made her mutter instead, 'He shouldn't have had to walk down to the Ruffinis the day before. They could have come up to the villa if there was any need to see them at all.'

'Not if he wanted to see Pratolino for himself,' Giles patiently pointed out. 'Now, let's be on our way; I'll get you back as quickly as I can.'

Little was said on the return journey, but they made such good time that lunch was still on the terrace table when they arrived. Jacqueline stared at her stepmother with an expression that seemed to ask how she could eat as if the day was normal, and then stalked off to her father's room without a word of greeting.

'She doesn't mean to be rude,' Joan suggested optimistically. 'She adores her father, and the rest of us don't matter very much!' Then she managed to smile at Giles and Jonathan. 'You need some lunch – I'll tell Lucia you're here.'

Giles waited until she was out of earshot and then smiled at his wife. 'There goes the woman who couldn't speak a word of

Italian three weeks ago. I take my hat off to you, Nell, as a language teacher.'

'Give Joan the credit,' she insisted. 'No one could have an apter pupil.'

The two men were helping themselves from the dishes Carlotta brought out when Jacqueline reappeared. 'I've been instructed to come and eat,' she announced. 'My father says he needs nothing at the moment – just to be left in peace to have his afternoon rest.'

She tried to sound offhand as usual, but, to Jonathan's now experienced ear, there was a note of hurt in her voice. In her absence he *had*, apparently, been well looked after, and she wasn't as indispensable as she'd thought.

'Your father's very glad to know you're back, I'm sure,' Jonathan heard himself say. 'He can snooze happily while you help us demolish Lucia's salami and mortadella.' Nell waited for her to reject a suggestion made by her brother, but Jacqueline sat down instead with a glance at him that almost held gratitude.

By now deeply curious to know how the stay in Milan had gone, Nell ambushed him in his room when lunch was over and found him emailing reports to London.

'Stop flicking keys, please, and talk to me,' she begged. 'I want to hear all about it.'

He launched into an account of Amanda Crichton's triumphant performance, to which Nell made the right comments before repeating her question. '*All* about it, I said. Why are you suddenly so anxious to bolster up Jacqueline's self-esteem? A work of supererogation, I'd have thought.'

He grinned at the phrase, typical of his sister's passion for the richness of the English language, but answered seriously. 'I suppose because I've got to know her a little better. She's a strange mixture of the insufferable and the defenceless! I treat her quite roughly, I'm afraid, but there are times when I want to give her a hug and say that I'm being cruel only to be kind!'

Nell looked at him with an anxiety in her face that he could easily identify and smile at.

'I'm not, by the way, in danger of being lured on to her siren's rock! Lovely though she is, my heart beats at its usual un-impressionable rate, and I'm afraid the lack of interest is entirely mutual. She has a poor opinion of men in general because too many of them have seen her as a way of getting near Frank, and at least one of her reasons for valuing Giles is that he's devoted to serving her father, not to getting something out of him.'

'Well, I have to think the better of her for that,' Nell admitted, 'but her affection for him is equalled, unfortunately, by her contempt for her stepmother, and that I can't forgive.'

'The subject of Joan also came up,' Jonathan said, 'and she got back here to discover that Frank's attitude towards his wife is not quite what it was – another blow as far as Jacqueline is concerned.' He smiled at his sister's expression. 'I agree she's still more nearly insufferable than anything else, but we might yet be able to help her grow up.'

'*You* perhaps, not *we*,' Nell insisted, 'seeing that she barely acknowledges I'm here, and clearly wishes I wasn't.'

'Don't blame her for that,' Jonathan said gently. 'She realizes that people can't help loving you. It's a gift she hasn't got, and she knows that too.'

Nell neatly changed the subject. 'Must you really go back to London? Sylvie rejoins us tomorrow and you're the only one of us with whom she feels truly *en rapport*!'

He smiled at the sisterly tit-for-tat and agreed that he could wait one more day and still be back in London before the shipment of scenery from Milan was due to arrive. She allowed him then to return to his emails and went downstairs.

Giles and Bertrand were in the office, she supposed, poring over plans; Joan was resting after their disturbed night; and Jacqueline had almost certainly taken possession of the pool. Disinclined to settle down to work, Nell considered delivering Bertrand's monastery designs to Father Pavese, but a long walk in the scorching mid-afternoon heat seemed to be what Beppe would certainly describe as Anglo-Saxon madness. Instead, she chose a seat in the shadiest part of the terrace and looked again at the drawings Bertrand had made – proof, if she needed it, of how brilliant an architect he was: everything there seemingly left unaltered, but made usable.

'May I see what you're looking at?' a voice spoke behind her.

She spun round to find Frank Middleton standing there, dressed still in pyjamas and robe, but otherwise looking much as usual. About to point out that the doctor had prescribed rest, she wasn't given the chance to speak.

'I've been lying in bed until I'm sick of it,' he said. 'Give me something to think about.' He settled himself beside her and, without argument that she knew would be useless, she passed him Bertrand's sketches.

'This is the monastery, now closed, that we went to look at the other day,' she explained. 'It's what Father Pavese and others hoped to convert into a home and school for deprived children. These sketches are Bertrand's idea of how it could be done. I was going to take them into Poggione this afternoon but decided on a cooler morning walk tomorrow instead.'

'Why not just knock all this down and put something purpose-built in its place?' Middleton suggested. 'More practical, and probably cheaper in the long run.'

'Bertrand doesn't think so,' she insisted gently. 'Added to that, these buildings are beautiful, in good repair, and they have an atmosphere of peace and serenity that we can't afford to lose.' She smiled suddenly. 'Say "poppycock" to that and I shall forget you're an invalid and shout at you, Sir Frank!'

He stared at her as a Great Dane might look at an impudent small terrier. But Nell's smile was one he hadn't often seen, and he answered quite mildly. 'I was actually going to say that peace and serenity might not suit a horde of slum children, certainly not the ones I've come across in Yorkshire. They're used to noise, not silence.'

'I'm sure they are, but shouldn't they have the chance to know that something else exists? And why not let them live in the middle of beauty, instead of a soulless modern box?'

He shook his head, rather regretfully. 'I told you once before: you're sentimental – a kind heart except when you're squaring up to me, but about as much sense as a newborn babe. Joan says you write books for children – I can see you might be quite good at that.'

He handed the drawings back, indicating that that part of the conversation was over.

'Your brother looked after Jacqueline in Milan – I've to thank him for that, seeing that he probably didn't much want to.'

At a loss to know how to answer, Nell said nothing at all, but, to her surprise, Middleton went on talking.

'I dare say you reckon she's been spoilt. If so, I'm to blame, not her stepmother. I wanted her to be content with Huddersfield, d'you see, not long to go running off as her mother did years ago. That's why I fixed on Giles – I knew he'd be able to handle her. Hard on you, of course, but I was thinking of her, not you.'

It was as nearly an apology as he could make, Nell realized, and it had cost him something to offer it. 'Thank you – I understand now,' she said simply.

Prompted by an untypical air of doubt about him, she then risked a question. 'Would it matter very much if she chose London? She's still your daughter, wherever she is, and she loves you very much. It's why she refuses to accept her stepmother – she wants it to be just you and her beating the rest of us! She might be happier settled in London – and Giles would still take care of her for you.' Nell lifted her hands in a little gesture of regret. 'I'm sorry – you didn't ask for my opinion. I speak too often without thinking.'

'Well, God help us when you really set your mind to it,' the man beside her said. 'You should wear some sort of warning placard – "appearances are deceptive".' He considered this for a moment and then plunged into another unexpected confession. 'I let Jacqueline grow up thinking that her stepmother's time for being useful was over. Joan was kind and loyal, of course, but, unlike the two of us, she didn't amount to much. The past few weeks have taught me something I needed to know: she amounts to rather a lot.'

'I think so too,' Nell said, smiling at him, 'and, if I'm right, you've come to terms with Italy as well; so perhaps you'll want to keep in touch with Sergio and Marco. They'd like you to know what happens at Pratolino.'

'Which, put another way, means that Nell Fanshawe reckons it's my duty to keep a fatherly eye on Marco from now on.'

She blushed for the accuracy of his guess and didn't know, when he got up and walked away into the house, whether he was angry or only amused. Left alone, she mulled over a conversation that she knew she wouldn't share, even with Giles. A moment of weakness had led a hard, self-confident man into giving away a lot about himself; all she could do for him in return was keep the knowledge to herself.

There was also her own unhappy situation to think about. Perhaps only loyalty to the family he served made Giles behave to Jacqueline as if the Cortona episode hadn't happened.

Nell didn't need him to explain that to treat Jacqueline differently in front of the others would be to humiliate her. But even if the flame of infatuation had burned itself out, what was left of their own relationship? He was a courteous, considerate room-mate who showed no regret that he could scarcely share her single bed. If passion was dead – and with it her longing for children of their own – then for her their marriage would be over. She needed more than an affectionate friendship with her husband . . . she needed to be loved. But, desperate not to show her need, she had reduced intimacy to a minimum, went to bed before he did, rose while he was still asleep, and wondered how much longer she could bear her 'convenient' marriage.

# Twenty-One

The following morning, about to set off for Poggione to deliver the monastery drawings to the *presbiterio*, it occurred to Nell to ask Bertrand if he would go with her. He was the person to discuss them with Father Pavese, not her. Since their last, intimate conversation she had avoided being alone with him, but this was different – a professional matter in which he was deeply interested. He agreed at once but on condition, he said, that he was allowed to drive them into the town.

'No inclination for a good, long walk?' Nell suggested, smiling at him.

'None at all,' Bertrand admitted frankly. 'Dear Nell, we don't have your strange English passion for travelling whenever possible on foot – so *en voiture*, madame, if you please!'

Laughing, she allowed herself to be overruled and got into the car, unaware of being observed.

It was Giles who watched them from the office window and tasted first the bile of envy suddenly rising in his throat, then the rage that took the place of envy. It was all wrong. To have one's wife admired by other men was a compliment in its way to oneself; to have her looking happy in the company of one particular man was something else again, and, in the case of Bertrand de la Tour, something that made him feel sick with anger and despair. He stood there for a long while after they'd driven away, trying to blame Nell, but it couldn't be done. The moment of truth had been reached and, with it, the knowledge that the pit of misery he was in was entirely of his own making.

He gave up the pretence of trying to work and sat down to wait for Frank Middleton. The time had come to make a choice: his life with Nell in one scale, a dazzling professional future in the other. Both he could not have, but he must choose without even knowing whether Nell had already been lost. He didn't consider what he would say when the moment arrived – the words would speak themselves, sealing what was to happen.

It was mid-morning when Middleton walked into the room, followed by Carlotta with their tray of coffee. He looked rested, Giles noted; almost with an air of unusual contentment about him, as if he, too, had taken a decision that needed making.

'Still no news yet from the Cortona lawyer?' he asked as they drank their coffee.

Giles shook his head. 'It will be any moment now, but it's out of his hands – I'm afraid the judge sets the timetable.' He fidgeted with the papers in front of him, carefully tidied them again, and then looked at the man he'd come to regard as true friend as well as employer.

'Frank, there's something I need to say,' he began unsteadily. 'I can't accept the job you were good enough to offer me. When things are settled here one way or the other and we return to London, I must go back to Marchants. I know it's a bad time to . . . to jump ship when you've been unwell, but you'll want to be looking around for someone else.'

There was a long, nerve-racking pause before Middleton spoke. 'Does your wife know that you're refusing?'

'No, I think she still expects that I'll accept. I finally decided not to just this morning. It's something else to apologize for – taking so long to say no.'

Middleton's gaze lingered on the younger man's face, noting its look of strain and tiredness. 'The apologies might come better from me,' he said unexpectedly. He got up to refill his coffee cup, leaving Giles to wonder what was coming next.

'I had an idea – guessed at by your wife – that didn't come off, but it gave her good reason to dislike me and Jacqueline. Between us we may have buggered up your marriage; if not, talk to Nell. I don't say she takes to me any better now, but at least we understand each other.'

Giles registered the unthinking use of her Christian name – that hadn't happened before – but steeled himself for what else had to be said. 'Your idea concerned Jacqueline, I assume. Well, the fact is that I'm the one who might have wrecked my marriage. I played the fool – only excusable if I was twenty years younger than I am. It's over now, but hurt has been done. Jacqueline will soon recover, I'm sure, but my relationship with Nell may not.'

'You didn't think to find out about that before turning me down?' Middleton asked.

'I did, of course, but I knew I had to make my choice first – Nell, or the job she'd hate me to take – *before* finding out whether I still had a marriage.'

The man watching him smiled. 'My own wife would tell me that I must hang on to a man who knows right from wrong – not many do nowadays. Time was when I wouldn't have listened to what she said. I didn't expect to come here and be shown by an Italian – Count or not – what I should have seen for myself: that my wife ought to be properly valued.'

'Maddening,' Giles agreed with a wry smile. He could have confessed that the same service rendered by a Frenchman was even harder to bear, but it would have cut too near the bone and hurt too much. Instead, he took refuge in matters of business. 'There are papers for you to sign and then I'll take them to Pratolino. Thereafter you can forget about those other two farms – they'll belong to the Ruffini family.'

Middleton scrawled his signature on the papers but shook his head. 'Thereafter nothing! Your dear wife informs me that I'm required to keep an eye on Marco in future. I mean to say no when she tells me what I've got to do, but the next minute I find myself, like now, signing on the dotted line!' He put down his cup and stood up. 'Talk to her, Giles; then I'll decide whether I need to accept your refusal or not.'

The visit to the *presbiterio* over, Nell and Bertrand were sitting in the sunlit square, sipping wine and watching Poggione life go by.

'Will that children's refuge ever come about?' Nell asked. 'There *must* be money somewhere – children's charities, government grants . . .'

'But tracking them down requires someone with a lot of time on his hands, Nell – that pleasant priest we've just seen is a busy man, I fancy,' Bertrand pointed out.

She nodded, then a beatific smile lit her face. 'Vittorio . . . he can't spend his entire life writing poetry!'

Bernard's shout of laughter startled a loitering pigeon, but he grew serious again. 'You never give in, do you?'

Then he fumbled in his pocket and pulled out a small leather box. 'Open it, please,' he asked.

Inside, resting in its velvet bed, she found a small gold crucifix on a cobweb-fine chain.

'It belonged to my mother. Since she died I've never found a woman I wanted to give it to until now. Will you have it, Nell?' Bertrand's quiet voice laid no pressure on her – she was free to refuse, he seemed to say.

She felt the sting of tears in her eyes and blinked them away. 'I shall wear it as soon as I get back to London,' she said unevenly, and she hid the little box in the pocket of her skirt. Her hand touched his for a moment, and then she tried to smile at him.

'What happens if Giles's Cortona deal goes through – must you stay much longer? I have the feeling that you want to get back to Paris.'

'Yes, I do. It's lovely here, a sort of Lotus land where it's always afternoon, but I miss my own city. I'd have to come back to check on progress, but surveyors and builders are in place if Giles confirms that work can start.'

He sipped his wine and then went slowly on. 'It's a great pity that we didn't get the original site. It's taken too long to find something else, and I'm not sure even Frank himself hasn't lost some of his original enthusiasm. Jacqueline is very bored with Tuscany, as is my wife, and it's time we all split up!' He stared at Nell's thin face, wanting to commit it to memory. 'I know you feel an attachment to this place, but perhaps you'll be glad to get back to London.'

'Relieved, anyway,' Nell had to admit. 'I hope I can come back to visit Sergio and Marco, but Giles and I have been treading water long enough. We need to go home and sort out our future.' She saw the expression on Bertrand's face, but shook her head at what she guessed he longed to say. 'We shan't forget the Villa Guidi, but you were right – it's time to leave Lotus land and get back to the real world.'

She said it with such gentle firmness that he knew the conversation was at an end – the last one that he would have with her alone – but there was nothing to be done; only pay for their wine and take her back to the villa.

They hadn't been absent for very long, but the moment they

stepped inside the house it was obvious that events had moved
on. Sylvie had torn herself away from Venice at last for one thing
– her luggage was sitting in the hall – but it was more than that:
a certain tension in the air suggested a change of some kind, and
out on the terrace a moment later it seemed as if the others gath-
ered there were waiting for them.

Bertrand had scarcely time to greet his wife before Jacqueline
made sure she was the one to break the news.

'Well, it's all off – now we can leave this dead and alive place
that I wish we'd never come to.'

Nell looked a question at Giles, but he waited for Frank
Middleton to explain.

'The Cortona estate is not for sale after all. The judge's decision went against the people we were dealing with – the lawyer
rang while you were out. That's our last hope gone.' He looked
across at Bertrand. 'Our beautiful hotel won't be built now. My
wife thinks we might have offended the spirits of this ancient place,
but she has a turn for the whimsical! I'm inclined to think myself
that I should stick to what I know about and leave beauty alone
– although I did mean it to serve a useful purpose here as well.'

There was a respectful silence for a moment, then Nell heard
herself speak the words that formed in her mind without conscious
thought or premeditation.

'Sir Frank, there's still something that can be done here
combining what you wanted to achieve – beauty plus usefulness.
We delivered Bertrand's plans for converting the closed monastery
into a children's home to Father Pavese this morning, but that's
as far as they will ever get unless he can find a benefactor.'
Struggling now, she made herself finish what she had to say. 'I
suppose you . . . you wouldn't consider that as an alternative to
the hotel?'

Before he could speak, Jacqueline was on her feet, beating
the table with her fists.

'You're right for once – he *wouldn't* consider it,' she shouted.
'Go and tell your precious priest to tear up his plans. We've already
had to keep your poor relations afloat. We're sick of your interference . . . in fact, of you being here at all – you weren't even
meant to come.' She had to stop at last for lack of breath and
her father could take charge.

'That's enough, lass. I'll decide what we do or don't do; you just need to apologize to a guest who *was* invited here.'

Eyes bright with angry tears, she stared back at him. 'I won't . . . I won't. She's got round you, but I hate her for spoiling everything.' She heard Sylvie give a pained sniff – this wasn't the sort of scene she was used to – and turned to glare at her instead. 'You'd better watch out, too, Madame de la Tour. Giles isn't enough for Mrs Fanshawe – she wants your husband as well!'

Pleased with this parting shot, Jacqueline kissed her fingers at them and walked away into the house.

For a frozen moment no one moved or even seemed to breathe. Then Nell, white-faced, managed to find her voice. 'I apologize for inflicting that on the rest of you – it's my besetting sin; I speak without thinking. But I didn't mean to upset Jacqueline so much.' She glanced at Giles but could read nothing in his face, and it was Jonathan who gave her hand a little comforting pat. But no one had decided what it would be safe to say before they heard the dialogue that went with anything Beppe and Lucia did together. It was the signal that lunch was being brought out; something about the day was still normal.

They must have heard Jacqueline's outburst but ignored it, either with perfect tact or with the Italian acceptance of drama as a normal ingredient of daily life.

'*La signorina non ha fame,*' Joan Middleton said bravely, seeing that Beppe had noticed her absence. '*Tutto va bene, grazie.*' Then she offered them all a tremulous smile. 'Let's eat, shall we? Lucia's spaghetti *alle vongole* won't wait for Jacqueline to decide she's hungry after all.'

Frank's hand touched her shoulder in a little gesture of gratitude, and they took their places round the table. Jonathan roused himself to ask Sylvie about the Fenice Theatre in Venice, finally rebuilt after its not so recent fire, and gradually a sort of normality reasserted itself. But it was a meal that no one enjoyed, for which they agreed to blame the day's increasing heat and almost unbearable humidity. They left the table as soon as they could and, like animals scenting danger, split up to hide themselves wherever they could rather than have to talk to each other.

Nell went straight to her usual garden refuge, but the paper she was drawing on stuck damply to her hand and she abandoned the attempt to work. No sound came from the direction of the swimming pool, and she walked there wondering whether, since no one was there, she could simply step out of her skirt and sandals and let herself into water that must at least be cooler than the stifling air.

But the decision didn't need to be made because a moment later two hands splayed out hard against her back and sent her toppling into the pool. She was conscious of falling, then of pain as her head hit the sharp edge of the diving board that jutted out across the water. There was a moment's awareness that she could do nothing to help herself, and then no sensation at all.

# Twenty-Two

The stone she was lying on was hard but warm against her wet skin. She thought about this for a moment, trying to work out what it meant. A voice above her head kept asking her to breathe deeply, open her eyes, say something. It was irritating when she had this problem of her own to solve. *Why* the warm stone under her back? *Back* . . . the word chimed in her mind, reviving a memory of strong hands planted against her, thrusting her into space. She remembered something else – she'd hit her head, could feel now that it hurt. Water dribbled out of her mouth, and someone gently wiped it away. The kindness insisted that she must see whose hand it was.

'Nell . . . Nell love, thank God you're all right.' The voice sounded strange, but she recognized Giles, even with anguish still written on his face. 'I heard Jacqueline cry out – she was trying to hold your head above water when I got here.'

It took an effort, but Nell managed to lift her hand and winced when it touched the bruise already swelling on her forehead. 'I hit the diving board when I fell in. Now I'm tired of lying here – I think I'd like to sit up.'

With his arm under her shoulders, she heaved herself up and, in this altered position, saw Jacqueline, holding what she recognized as her sketchbook, now sodden beyond saving.

'It's spoiled – I'm sorry,' the girl said. But her eyes, enormous in a face that was pale beneath its tan, seemed oddly full of fear rather than regret.

'Sweetheart, did you feel ill?' Giles asked. 'Is that why you fell?'

The question seemed to spark such tension in the air that Nell was suddenly sure of the reason for it. Jacqueline was waiting for her to answer. 'I remember standing here and thinking how unbearably hot it was, but not much else except banging my head.' She made herself smile at the girl. 'Thank you for helping to fish me out!' Then she turned back to Giles. 'I'm all right now, but I'd like to lie on a soft bed in a cool, dark room for a little while.'

He helped her up, and they slowly climbed the steps of the terrace. Jacqueline was told to fetch her stepmother, and Giles and Joan peeled off Nell's soaked clothes and wrapped her in a cotton robe. Then, with pills administered and her bruise anointed with arnica, Joan insisted that she be left to rest.

'It's all she needs now,' she said, gently shooing Giles from the room, but her eyes still looked anxious. 'What a dreadful day – can anything else happen, I wonder?'

'A storm, almost certainly, and God knows we need it,' Giles suggested.

'What happened at the pool? Did Nell faint because of the heat?'

Giles hesitated. 'She doesn't seem to remember, but the temperature on top of that scene before lunch was enough to tax anyone.'

Joan touched his arm in a little gesture of apology. 'I'm sure she's all right, my dear, and I hope you know that Jacqueline was speaking out of some ill-will all her own. Nell is like my own daughter, and Frank has become more fond of her than he knows how to admit.'

Giles suddenly spoke of something else. 'Did you know about the job he offered me? Apart from how Nell feels about it, having his daughter hate my wife doesn't seem to make for a workable arrangement.'

Joan shook her head. 'Frank would tell you to leave Jacqueline out of it – she's our problem, not yours. Now, go and find Jonathan before he hears about the accident. Assure him that Nell's all right.'

'Yes, ma'am!' Giles smiled at her, convinced now that his wife had been right all along. Joan Middleton had never deserved contempt from anyone.

Run to earth across the courtyard, his brother-in-law was locked in battle with the Count over the music-dramas of Richard Wagner. He delivered his message and then went back to the office. There was work to be done, and he desperately needed something to occupy his mind while he waited for Nell to rest. But the threatened storm broke at last, and he spent the next hour watching it from the window – its sound and fury fitting background music to a day he would never forget.

With the air finally cooled and sweet again after the rain, he

went outside to breathe in its freshness and see the garden almost
visibly coming alive again after the deadening heat; then he climbed
the stairs to check on Nell.

He found her in her usual seat by the window, with only the
livid bruise on her forehead to remind him of what had happened.

'I had to come and watch the storm,' she confessed, smiling
at him.

'Me too, from the office window. You look all right – *are* you?'

'Myself again,' she insisted.

'Then perhaps you feel strong enough to tell me what happened
this afternoon. I need to know, Nell.' He saw the distress in her
face and went on himself. 'Jacqueline "happened" to be there
when you fell in – shall I guess that she was right behind you
at the time? I saw her face when she waited for you to explain
. . . she was terrified of you accusing her.'

Nell gave up trying to evade the truth. 'All right, someone
pushed me – Jacqueline, I think, because her perfume is so recog-
nizable. But I'm quite sure she only set out to make me look
ridiculous or to give me a fright. She never for a moment dreamed
that I'd bump my head on the diving board, and she did, in all
probability, save me from drowning.'

Haunted by the moment when they'd pulled Nell out of the
water, Giles buried his face in his hands. When he lifted his head,
she saw how anguished he looked. 'She hates you because of me
– it's as much my blame as hers.'

'We'll blame everyone who's ever crossed her if you like,
including me!' Nell suggested. 'Frank spoiled her in the hope of
keeping her content – he admitted it, poor man, not even being
sure that it will work.'

'It won't – sooner or later she'll go her own way, whatever
indulgences he pours into her lap.'

Nell lifted the hand that held hers to her cheek. 'Promise me
something, please. No one is to know what happened this afternoon, least of all Frank or Joan.'

Giles nodded and saw her smile. He stared at her face, known
but not sufficiently loved. Blinded by Jacqueline's so obvious
beauty, he'd overlooked his wife's much more elusive attraction.

'My dear, I've been such a complete and abject fool,' he said
unevenly. 'You're my only love, the true companion of my heart,

and I didn't need this afternoon to show me what I was in danger of losing. I told Frank this morning that I was going back to Marchants.'

'What did he say?' Nell asked.

'That I should speak to you – pointless, of course, when I knew what you felt about his job. He seemed to think the two of you had reached some sort of understanding, so I couldn't bring myself to say that you'd had more than enough of the Middleton family. The sad thing is that he now likes *you* rather a lot – Joan confirmed that this afternoon.' Giles put the subject aside for one that seemed to matter much more now. 'Nell, I have to ask about Bertrand. I saw you drive away together this morning – couldn't miss how happy you both looked.'

She hesitated for a moment, then got up and crossed the room to a chest of drawers. A small box was in her hand when she came back.

'He gave me this.' She offered Giles the little crucifix. 'It belonged to his mother, and I promised to wear it for her. They had a wretched life because his father abandoned them, but she worked herself to death to give Bertrand the start he needed. He loved her very much. He and I are very glad to have known each other, but now he will go back to Paris with Sylvie, and I can't wait to go back to London with you.'

She leaned forward and gently kissed his mouth. 'Take Frank's job, please. If he's going to lose Jacqueline, he can't afford to lose you as well.'

Giles's arms enfolded her and held her close, telling her that passion wasn't dead; the marriage of convenience was over. 'Time to go downstairs,' he said with great reluctance. 'Do you feel up to it, sweetheart, or would you rather stay here?'

She smiled and shook her head. 'I feel up to anything except another swim in the pool!'

But that reminded him of the afternoon's horror, and something else that needed mentioning. 'Nell, your sketchbook was ruined – all those enchanting drawings . . . can you redo them from memory?'

'I shan't even try. We shan't forget the Villa Guidi, but I find I don't want to write about it, after all.'

She sounded too definite for him to argue, and he simply said instead that it was time to get dressed. 'Please God, it will be a peaceful dinner,' he added fervently. 'We've had enough drama for one day.'

The meal, if anything, was quieter than usual, all of them taking care not to ruffle the uneasy calm. But when they were back in the *salone*, rather than on the cool, rain-washed terrace, Frank Middleton suddenly put down his coffee cup and stood up – they were about to be addressed, it seemed.

'Listen, please,' he asked gravely. 'Joan and I would like to go home – earlier than expected, I know, but there is nothing left to stay for now. Giles still has matters to clear up, so he and Nell will be here for another day or two. Bertrand, you and Sylvie stay too, of course, as long as you like, though I suspect you're wanting to get back to Paris. Jonathan is leaving tomorrow anyway.'

'You haven't mentioned me.' Jacqueline's voice broke the silence. 'What am I supposed to do?'

Middleton smiled at her. 'You come home with us, lass, of course. We've got seats booked on the same flight as Jonathan tomorrow.'

With a sense of sad inevitability, Nell knew what would come next. On her feet now, Jacqueline confronted her father. 'If "home" means Huddersfield, I'm not coming with you.' She spoke with a quiet certainty that was more effective than the morning's histrionics had been. 'You can't force me to get on that plane.'

About to make the mistake of asking what she would do instead, her father was halted by the sight of Jonathan getting to his feet. Apparently unaware that no one else was capable of moving hand or foot, he strolled across the room to where Jacqueline stood.

'If you're set against Yorkshire, I've got another idea. It would mean being a very small fish in a rather large pool – not what you're used to, I fancy.'

She stared at him, not sure whether he was friend or foe. 'What idea?'

'I think you need something to do that interests you – not your father's business empire. You seem to have a passion for clothes: why not learn about them? London's design studios are the most inventive in the world, and I have friends who could get you enrolled in one of them. You'd have to work hard, and they'd throw you out if you didn't.' Then he suddenly turned to her father. 'I'm speaking out of turn, Sir Frank – what do *you* think of the idea?'

'It seems to be a family failing, speaking out of turn,' he said grimly. 'If it means my daughter living on her own in London, I don't think much of it at all.'

'On her own, but not without friends,' Jonathan insisted. 'Nell and Giles and I would be there to keep an eye on her.'

Jacqueline ran across the room and clutched Middleton's arm.

'Let me do it, please . . . *please* let me, Pa. I'd work hard, I promise. Everybody says I have an eye for clothes, but I need to be taught.' For the first time in her life, she appealed to her stepmother. 'Help me persuade him. I need to leave home, but that doesn't mean I won't be coming back.'

Joan looked across at her husband and gave a little nod. 'Let her go, Frank,' she said quietly. 'You'll see her often in London, and our dear friends will take care of her.'

'Well, you'll come home first,' he stated, admitting defeat. 'We've to see if Jonathan *can* get you enrolled; then there'd be a flat to find, money to sort out. And your stepmother's a bad traveller – she'll need you with us tomorrow.'

'I'll come . . . of course I will,' Jacqueline promised, smearing away sudden tears. 'Jonathan needs help too, with only one good arm still.' She went back to where he still stood and reached up to kiss his cheek. 'I shan't stay a very small fish for long, you know.'

'No, I don't suppose you will,' he agreed, and, on that note of harmony, they all tacitly agreed that an eventful day was finally over and they could retire to bed.

# Twenty-Three

Bertrand and Sylvie were the first to leave the following morning. With Beppe standing by, and Sylvie saying goodbye to the Middletons, Nell found little to add to what she and Bertrand had already said to each other. But he could see the glint of a gold chain in the open collar of her shirt, and she touched it briefly.

'I told Giles it had belonged to your mother,' she found herself wanting to explain. 'He understands why I value it.'

'I'm glad,' he said gravely. 'That way it does no harm.' Then his odd, bony face broke into a smile. 'Go with God, my dear Nell.'

She managed to return the lovely Spanish farewell. 'And you also.'

A moment later Sylvie had been handed into the car by Beppe, and Bertrand climbed in beside her. Beppe gave his usual departing toot on the horn and they drove out of the courtyard.

Lunch was earlier that day, so that soon afterwards Beppe in one car and Giles driving the other could take the Middletons and Jonathan to Pisa airport for the afternoon flight to London.

'Promise me we won't lose touch,' Joan pleaded as she kissed Nell goodbye.

'Friends don't,' she was told firmly, 'and in any case Sergio and Marco are expecting us all back for the *vendemmia*.' It was harder to know how to say goodbye to Jacqueline, but Nell held out a friendly hand and at least felt it gripped tightly for a moment. Then it was Frank Middleton standing in front of her.

'Giles is taking the job, but I expect you knew that already,' he said, not expecting to be contradicted. 'No hard feelings, I hope, Nell?'

'None at all,' she confirmed with a smile that drew an answering one from him and then a vigorous farewell pat on the shoulder. He next called his family to order, and Nell was free to hug her brother.

'Be careful, won't you? Don't get too involved . . .'

His cheerful grin halted her. 'Fear not, love. Our tiresome little signorina knows who's in charge! I'm prepared to swear you'll hardly know her in a month or two.'

'Ever the optimist,' she suggested, 'but heaven knows I hope you're right.'

With the Count, who'd come to join in the farewells, she watched the two cars drive away, and then they both returned to the terrace and the fresh coffee Carlotta brought out. Vittorio Guidi looked sad, and Nell feared that, without his Donna Joanna, he would now sink back into the lonely isolation from which he'd been briefly rescued.

'You are all leaving sooner than planned,' he commented mournfully. 'It means that Beppe and Lucia can have a little holiday, of course, but it will seem very quiet without you.'

'Quietness was what you used to enjoy,' she pointed out, 'and Lucia says you have American tenants expected later on.'

'Yes, with teenaged children!' he agreed in the tones of a man expecting the worst. Then his voice changed. 'I heard about your fall in the pool, and I can see that you hurt yourself. If the sketch-book is really ruined, could I not send you photographs of the little statues?'

She was touched by his kindness, but shook her head. 'I'm afraid *The Magic Garden* won't get written after all – I couldn't make it come to life in my mind. Perhaps too much else was going on!'

His nod seemed to agree. 'There were some changes, I think – some of them for the better. Donna Joanna went away happier than she arrived, and you also, Nell, are content again. I, on the other hand, am left a little sad, and Bertrand has gone without something of great value to him.' He saw the colour mount in Nell's thin cheeks and gently touched her hand. 'The onlooker sees most of the game – isn't that an English expression?'

She agreed that it was, then turned the conversation to a less personal subject. 'If you'd be willing not to be an onlooker for a change, there's something you could get very involved in.' She went briefly over the story of the shutdown monastery and Father Pavese's need for help. 'He has a parish to run and a frail, elderly father to look after,' she finished up. 'More than that, he needs influential help, someone who knows who to approach for money – someone with what at home we call "clout"!'

'Clout!' Vittorio savoured the unfamiliar word, and then his shy smile appeared. 'If you think I have it, I must try to use it in such a worthwhile cause. And I must also now keep in touch with my neighbours. I have you to thank, dear Nell, for knowing the Ruffinis.'

'While I have to thank Sir Frank for bringing us here at all,' Nell pointed out. 'Otherwise I might never have known that Sergio and Marco existed, or learned the rest of my grandmother's story.' She smiled suddenly. 'I hope I didn't ask Francesca's ghost to put a jinx on the hotel project, but it *was* right that it shouldn't be built; it wasn't what was needed here. Marco's plans are a much better idea.'

For the first time she heard her companion laugh out loud, and he was still smiling when he got up to return to his own wing of the house.

Left alone, Nell relaxed thankfully in the peace of a garden miraculously rejuvenated by the previous day's rain. Her hands were occupied with uprooting weeds, but her thoughts were else-where, concerned with the past weeks' complicated mixture of pleasure and pain. Surely no other short period of their lives had been so crucial in deciding what would happen next. Did she imagine it in this haunted garden or was Francesca's ghost standing beside her murmuring, 'What did you expect, *cara* – to come here and *not* find yourselves at the mercy of our old Etruscan gods?'

She was still outside, reluctant to say goodbye to a place she'd come to love, when Giles came looking for her. His tired face was no surprise; his passengers on the long drive to the airport had been Jacqueline and Jonathan, and she could imagine that the journey hadn't been a silent one.

'Safely delivered to the plane at least,' she commented, 'but does my dear, foolhardy brother understand what he's taken on?'

Giles answered with certainty, aware of the anxiety beneath her question. 'My dear, he understands perfectly, and Jacqueline is well aware that for the first time in her life she has to toe someone else's line.' He wiped a smear of dirt from his wife's cheek and smiled at her. 'Nell, I don't know about you but I can't wait to get home. If I get a move on with clearing things up, there's no reason why we can't make tomorrow afternoon's flight. How does that sound to you?'

'It sounds fine,' she agreed, 'provided we can fit in a visit to the farm to say goodbye there.'

'A quick wash and a clean shirt, then we could go now,' Giles suggested. 'I'd like a walk after being cooped up in the car for hours.'

They were made very welcome by Sergio and Marco, and pressed to share their supper, but they had to refuse, knowing that Lucia was already preparing food for them. Still, there was time for a glass of wine and much talk of future plans, and they were only allowed to leave after promising to return without fail in time to take part in the *vendemmia*.

Climbing the track again, Giles referred to the change in Marco. 'He's a different man already. I'll lay you even money, Nell, that dreams of an ideal communist society are fast fading from his mind. Another year or two and his earnest comrades will have been forgotten altogether.'

'But not his principles, I think,' Nell insisted. 'He'll remain the idealist he is now. What I hope *will* change is his lack of a wife. Sergio can't live for ever and then Marco will be lonely.' She turned to look enquiringly at Giles. 'Should we point him in Carlotta's direction . . . would that be permissible?'

Forbidding himself to smile, Giles agreed that it would, and they walked the rest of the way in contented silence. Lucia's delicious prawn risotto was ready when they got back, made still more enjoyable for being eaten by themselves for the first time since they'd arrived at the villa. But when coffee was on the table, Giles heard Nell give a little sigh.

'Too quiet, my love?' he asked anxiously. 'Too much of an anticlimax to end our visit?'

Nell shook her head. 'Anything but! I'm glad we can say goodbye to this lovely place so peacefully. But I *was* drawing up a sort of emotional balance sheet . . . so much profit, so much loss. I think that's how it's been for all of us.'

He hesitated, not sure what it would be safe to say. 'Well, if it's a game that two can play, I'll begin with Frank and Joan. He's losing Jacqueline but gaining a wife he knows he values after all. Joan's gain is obvious, but has there also been loss for her?'

Nell took a moment to answer. 'Some, I think; there'd be more if she thought Vittorio was really left hurt, but she hasn't a high enough opinion of herself for that.'

'So what about the Count?'

'Plunged in gentle melancholy,' Nell said with a smile. 'Exactly how a poet should feel! But I rely on Father Pavese to keep him busy in future – he isn't going to be allowed to sink into seclusion again.'

Giles detected her hand at work here, but didn't say so; something more painful had to be faced. 'I'm afraid there's nothing gentle about Bertrand's sadness.' He stared sombrely at Nell. 'This *isn't* a game we're playing, unfortunately. I can't help knowing that *he* won't forget you, or you *him*. I watched you saying goodbye this morning and it hurt, for both of you.'

She didn't deny it. 'Yes, it hurt; but that will fade. Then we shall be left with the pleasure of having met. Sylvie will help, I think, by valuing Bertrand properly in future, and I shall have you – all I really want.'

Giles reached out to take her hand and lift it to his mouth. 'There's been little profit here for you, my love,' he said unsteadily. 'I can't excuse my madness, but I *am* sane again now, and I love you more than life itself.'

Nell's smile embraced him. 'Francesca wouldn't have been surprised that we had to come here to find that out.'

He nodded, but had no time to put agreement into words because Beppe now unexpectedly reappeared, this time with an envelope in his hand which he laid on the table.

'From *il Signore*,' he explained. 'He gave it to me for you at the *aeroporto*, Signor Giles. I was to present it after dinner.'

'Trust Frank to remember in the nick of time something he thinks we've forgotten!' Giles commented when they were alone again. He idly slit open the envelope and two pieces of paper fell out. A glance at the smaller one made his face change.

'Good God,' he said in a stunned voice.

'Something's wrong . . . *still*? Oh, those blasted Etruscan gods again,' Nell muttered despairingly. 'Why won't they let us alone!'

But Giles, scarcely listening, was reading Frank's note. 'Listen to this,' he demanded. 'It concerns you too.'

*Dear Giles,*

*With the hotel project abandoned, I reckoned my dream of doing*
*something useful here was over too. Buying a defunct monastery*
*as an alternative wouldn't have occurred to me but for your dear*
*wife. You can tell her that turning it into a children's home seems*
*much more useful to me than having it house a bunch of old men*
*chanting psalms all day long!*

*The Count's lawyer gave me the asking price for Carmanuolo*
*– the enclosed euro-cheque should cover most of the conversion cost*
*as well. Sorry to give you more work when you thought you were*
*ready to leave, but you must blame Nell.*

*See you soon,*
*Yours,*
*Frank*

Nell didn't bother to look at the cheque; she was still staring at
the note in Giles's hand. 'When he saw me with Bertrand's sketches,
he said the best thing would be to just pull the building down.
I thought he meant it. What an extraordinary man he is.'

'Did you know that he and Joan had a son who died?' Giles
asked.

'Joan told me. Perhaps we owe this to that little boy.' Nell
stared at her husband. 'What happens now?'

'We see Pavese in the morning. I guess that a trust will have
to be set up; that needn't take long to get started, but I understand now why Frank thought we'd have to stay on!' He looked
at Nell, but saw her following some train of thought of her own.
'What are you hatching now, I wonder?'

'Not hatching exactly, only wondering whether, when the
school is ready, it can be dedicated to Frank's little son, and to
those schoolboys who died in Poggione's square.'

'We'll suggest it tomorrow,' Giles promised, and found Nell
now looking anxiously at him.

'Will you be honest with me, please?' she asked. 'Jacqueline
said I interfered, and Frank once suggested I should wear a placard
warning people of danger! *Do* I make a nuisance of myself . . .
badger those around me?'

Tempted to smile, he realized that she was in earnest.
'Sweetheart, never that. You just remind me sometimes of a lovely

golden retriever I had as a child; when she wanted something, she simply nudged me gently with her nose – it always did the trick!'

'Well, at least it sounds better than badgering.' Then Nell's worried expression faded. 'It's hard to think of Frank as an angel of grace, but it's certainly how Father Pavese will see him. Think of his face tomorrow when we give him his benefactor! Oh Giles, I could dance for pure joy.'

Her husband stood up and gave a little bow. 'I wonder if I might have the pleasure of the next waltz, Mrs Fanshawe?'

Trying not to laugh, Nell also got to her feet. 'Charmed, I'm sure,' she said primly, and was swept into his arms.

Coming to clear away the coffee cups, Beppe halted in the doorway and retreated silently to the kitchen.

'The English *are* mad,' he told his wife. 'I've often thought so; now I know for certain. Signor Giles and Signora Nell are *dancing* round the terrace.'

'*Amore*, they dance because they're happy – why does that make them mad?' Lucia wanted to know.

'Because, wife of my heart, there is no *music* – not one single note!'

She smiled and patted his cheek in the eternal gesture of a woman trying to forgive the incurable stupidity of her man. '*Caro*, try to understand,' she begged. 'You can't hear the music, but they *can*.'

Beppe thought about this for a moment, and then his thin, brown face broke into a smile. 'Then that is all right,' he said. 'In that case, they shall be allowed to dance all night if they want to.'